FROM "DUEL IDENTIES" BY DAVID LUBAR

"I don't know about this," Danny said.

"I don't either." I sighed and tried to hold on to the image I'd started with—me as a cool guy with mask and sword, fencing away while the clash of steel against steel rang through the air. It wasn't easy.

We left the locker room and headed for the girl's gym. Yup—one more indignity. The basketball players got the boy's gym, the swimmers got the pool at the YMCA, the wrestlers got the exercise room, and we got stuck sharing the floor with the clog dancing club.

"Okay, team, line up," Mr. Sinclair called.

FORGE BOOKS EDITED BY
M. JERRY WEISS & HELEN S. WEISS

From One Experience to Another
Lost and Found

To Marcia + Eli,

LOST AND FOUND

AWARD-WINNING AUTHORS SHARING REAL-LIFE EXPERIENCES THROUGH FICTION

Enjoy!

edited by
M. Jerry Weiss
& Helen S. Weiss

May you have many happy years together!
M. Jerry Weiss

FORGE®
A Tom Doherty Associates Book / New York

LOST AND FOUND

A Forge Book
Published by Tom Doherty Associates, LLC
175 Fifth Avenue
New York, NY 10010

www.tor.com

Forge® is a registered trademark of Tom Doherty Associates, LLC.

ISBN: 0-812-56866-4

First edition: August 2000
First mass market edition: August 2001

Printed in the United States of America

0 9 8 7 6 5 4 3 2 1

We dedicate this book to our many author and illustrator friends who have created a treasury of memorable stories and pictures. These very talented people are responsible for promoting a lifelong love of reading among people of all ages.

CONTENTS

ACKNOWLEDGMENTS

We are grateful to the many author friends who contributed their talents to this volume.

Many thanks to our agent, Mary Lou Brady.

Once again we appreciate the interest and efforts of two very good friends at Tor/Forge Books: Jonathan Schmidt and Kathleen Doherty.

NOTE TO THE READER

Dear Reader,

The most often asked question of authors is: "Where do you get your ideas?" We have wondered about that also. Much to our surprise we have found out that the variety of sources is quite remarkable.

Throughout the years we have learned that authors eavesdrop while riding in subways or trains, in buses and on planes, or even while walking down a street. Some authors carry a notebook and jot down just enough notes to remind them of what they have heard. Then they develop a filing system from which they draw upon their ideas.

Other authors have drawn upon their own experiences. Paul Zindel and Mel Glenn, for example, were teachers and remembered certain students and events. Joyce Hansen, also a teacher, found her story while conducting a writing workshop. Tamora Pierce recalls her experience as a housemother in a group home for teenage girls. Eleanora Tate has a fascination with snakes. Rich Wallace and Joan Abelove remember incidents in their lives as students. Something unusual brings out the story by David Lubar; a visit to a zoo triggered a story by Lois Metzger. Incidents at home gave wings for the writings by Shelley Stoehr and Mary Ann McGuigan. And Jon Scieszka recalls a book once read that triggered the idea for his unusual piece. Adele Griffin remembers those popular girls' magazines that featured glamorous models and the ways one could look just like them: the right hair style, the right lipstick, the right clothes. What about the right figure?

So, you see, you can look to your own life experiences for inspiration and ideas. These, with a little imagination, will carry you far in creating stories, essays, poetry, short stories, even novels and/or plays. Look at the different genres you can explore—horror, mystery, humor, fantasy, science fiction, human relationships, etc. You will be surprised at the number of stories you have to tell.

M. Jerry Weiss
Helen S. Weiss

LOST
AND
FOUND

Duel Identities

David Lubar

My files are filled with short stories inspired by small experiences and observations. The slightest oddness can strike a spark that sends me rushing to the word processor (unless there's something good on TV at the time). Usually, I take that oddness and create a fantasy or horror tale. But when I sat down to write a story for this collection, something interesting happened. I intended to play by the rules and start with one small experience. But as I dug into the murky depths of my high school memories, lifting chunks of experience the way the police raise abandoned cars from a river, two long-lost incidents broke the surface. Between them lay a season of other memories.

So, excuse me for going overboard, but this story contains more personal experiences than anything I've ever written. Sadly, the opening incident is true. Amazingly, so is the final incident. At least, most of it. As for the portion in the middle, much of it is based on experience. But I didn't hesitate to change the things that needed to be changed. Fiction isn't about telling what happened. It's about telling what is true. Enjoy.

I committed my first act of self-destruction less than five minutes into third period. We were sitting in the bleachers while Mr. Cadutto spelled out the basic facts of gym class to us brand spanking new freshmen. After explaining how many points we got for taking a shower and how many points we lost for forgetting our gym clothes, Mr. Cadutto said, "Okay. We're gonna pick four team leaders. You'll help set things up, so you won't get to do no calisthenics."

Whoa. That caught my attention. *Miss calisthenics.* My heart leaped at the opportunity to avoid having my heart leap. I joined the hand wavers, though I noticed that none of my fellow overachievers from first period honors English had entered this particular lottery. I'd already figured out that *honor* was an odd word around here. From the varsity jackets of the crowds in the hallway to the huge trophy case that faced the main entrance, it was obvious that honor was paid more to the body than the mind at Kennedy High.

Mr. Cadutto scanned us like a rancher at a beef auction. "You can't be no leader unless you go out for at least two sports."

Half the hands dropped. Mine remained airborne. Despite an inherited lack of bulk or speed or power, I did have two sports in my extracurricular plans. One just for the heck of it, but the other because it had entered my dreams in the hazy days of childhood, and remained there ever since.

Mr. Cadutto pointed to Bruno Haskins, up at the top of the bleachers, "Football and wrestling, right, Haskins?" he growled.

"Right, Coach."

Mr. Cadutto waved Bruno down. I sensed a rigged election. The gym teacher obviously already knew the star athletes in our class.

Bruno jogged to the bottom of the bleachers, making each row bounce under his weight. Mr. Cadutto selected Kyle Barrister next, and then Mookie Lahasca, two other champion jocks. Three down, one to go. He scanned us again, then frowned. I guess the jock gene pool had dried up too fast. He stared right at me. His brow creased with a puzzled expression.

"You," he barked, pointing one large sausage of a finger in my direction. He ran his eyes over my imposing seventy-eight-pound frame. "Wrestling?"

No way. There was zero appeal in the thought of having my body tied in knots like a rawhide dog chew. I shook my head.

"Track?" he asked, with a touch of disdain.

Another shake.

"Swimming?"

Nope.

"So what's your two sports?"

I uttered three innocent words. "Fencing and tennis."

There was dead silence for about nine-millionths of a second. Then the dam burst. Laughter splashed over me like acid rain, spewing from the mouth of every classmate, followed by waves of comments.

"Wow, tough guy!"

"Freakin' retard . . ."

"You forgot ballet."

"Jerk . . ."

Bruno cackled so hard he started choking. "Fencing," he sputtered between coughs.

"Coach said sports," Mookie shouted up at me, "not farts."

I knew exactly how the Wicked Witch of the West felt as she melted into a puddle of green ooze.

Mr. Cadutto, who should have been the adult in all of this, snorted like an ox that had just heard a really great joke. After he'd had a good chuckle, I guess he realized he should respond to my request. He regarded me with the sort of combined pity and loathing generally reserved for humans who've somehow managed to cover themselves with their own dung. He opened his mouth. Then he closed it. Then he opened it again. Finally, he shook his head and scanned the bleachers for other options.

My classmates continued to share their thoughts with me.

"Cool sports, Tarbell."

"Hey, if you add hopscotch, you can be a three-letter man."

"You scared to play a real sport?"

"Maybe he's afraid he'll break a nail."

"What a dork."

Apparently, there's a hierarchy of respect among sports. I should have known. I should have kept my mouth shut. I'm such an idiot.

After the fourth leader was selected, our new captains chose teams for volleyball. I was picked dead last. That had never happened in junior high. Even Hippo Schwartz got called before me. So did Billy Esterbridge, who by my estimate had failed in eight thousand consecutive attempts to serve the ball over the net. At least my humiliation had allowed others to climb briefly out of the muck engulfing the lowest of the low.

As the game started, I realized the full extent of my mistake.

"Fencing sucks," one of my teammates said as I walked past him.

"En garde," another said, jabbing me in the back with a finger.

Everyone who got within range took a poke. By the end of the period, I felt like an acupuncture practice dummy.

"Well, you're screwed," Danny Horvath said to me as we trudged into the locker room.

I could always count on Danny for moral support. That's what best friends are for. But he was right. For the next four years, or the rest of my life—whichever came first—I'd be known as the fencing dork. After a quick shower—far be it from me to miss a chance to improve my grade—I got dressed and slunk off through the locker room door.

"Fencing?" The mocking squawk echoed in the corridor.

Oh, no. I knew that voice. I kept walking.

"Fencing?" Louder this time.

"Ouch!" I spun around as I felt a sharp poke in the back. Trent Muldoon—he of the single eyebrow and single-celled brain—sneered at me.

"Yeah, fencing," I said. "It's a sport."

"For girls." Trent knocked my books from my hand, then sprinted down the hallway.

I thought about racing after him, leaping on his back, dragging him to the ground, and pounding him into a mass of quivering jelly. It might, just barely, have been possible. We were close to the same height. On the other hand, he was a wrestler—which meant he knew a lot more about fighting than I did.

Freshman survival rule #1: Never take someone on at his own game. But adrenaline can do wonders. Mothers have lifted cars off of trapped infants. Men have chewed their way out of steel cages. Teenage boys have eaten liver and onions. Well, maybe nothing that extreme. Still, with enough adrenaline behind my attack, I figured I could get in a punch or two. After which, he'd probably toss me on the ground and wrap me up in a wrestling hold so tight it would give me a firsthand chance to view my lower intestines from the inside. Besides, Trent had a lot of buddies. Large, stupid, mean buddies. I'd save revenge for another day.

I gathered my books.

"Scott, you sure about this fencing thing?" Danny asked as he came out of the locker room.

I'd thought I was—before learning the results of the fencing popularity poll. Now, I wasn't so sure. But the damage had already been done. If I didn't go out, I'd be more than just a wimpy dork. I'd be a wimpy dork quitter. "Yeah," I told Danny. "I'm gonna fence."

"The only ones who go out for fencing are kids who want a varsity letter and can't make any other team. Too weak to wrestle, too short for basketball, too dense for swimming . . ."

"I don't care," I told him. Scenes flashed through my head; musketeers with flashing rapiers, Jedi Knights with light sabers, Inigo Montoya in *The Princess Bride*, John Steed and Emma Peel—thank goodness for *Avengers* videos—Antonio Banderas and Catherine Zeta-Jones. Despite the opinion of the general population, fencing was way beyond cool. I just wished I wasn't the only one on the planet who felt that way.

"And it's a lot more than a sport," I added. "There's centuries of tradition. There's honor. There's spirit."

Danny yawned. "Yeah, sure. Whatever. Fencing is wonderful. Whoopee. I'm happy for you. Come on. Let's get out of here."

I followed him down the hall.

Life dragged on. Football season came and went. Finally, it was time for winter sports. After school, on the first day of sign-ups, I rushed to the gym.

I pushed my way through a thick, noisy mob clustered around Mr. Cadutto at the wrestling table. Other crowds buzzed around basketball and swimming sign-ups.

Across the gym, I spotted the fencing table. It was as uncrowded as a hot dog stand at a vegetarian convention. I walked over.

"Mr. Sinclair?" I asked, recognizing the physics teacher.

He nodded and smiled. "Yes. I'm the new fencing coach."

"What happened to Mr. Billings?" From what I'd heard, he'd always been the coach.

"He got married during the summer. His wife wants him to spend more time at home. So, like that, no fencing coach." Mr. Sinclair shrugged.

I realized a new coach wouldn't be bad, since he wouldn't have any favorites from last season. I picked up a pen and started filling out the sign-up form.

An older kid, a senior, I think, walked up. "Hey, Mr. Sinclair. I heard you were coaching us this year. Have you fenced much?"

"To tell the truth, I've never fenced," he said.

My hand stopped halfway through writing my last name.

"However, if I may boast, I'm quite a competent chess player." Mr. Sinclair grinned modestly. "If you can play chess, you can play any sport. Besides, nobody else wanted to coach. They were going to cancel the team. So I volunteered."

Oh, boy.

A couple more kids joined us at the table, including Billy Esterbridge from my gym class. I glanced over at the wrestlers. They looked like a magazine ad for a health club. So did the swimmers. Not the fencers. We looked like a poster for some unpleasant childhood disease that caused the body to either shrivel or bloat.

Much to my surprise, I saw Danny weaving his way through the crowd.

"Aren't you afraid of being seen with us dorks?" I asked.

Danny shrugged and picked up a pen. "Hey, you made it sound like too much fun to miss."

"Yeah. It'll do wonders for your status," I told him. "I've heard the junior and senior girls love fencers almost as much as they love the AV geeks."

"Hey," Billy said. "Cut it out. I like the audio-visual club. Without us, there'd be no intraschool dissemination of information."

"Relax," Danny said. "Scott was just kidding."

"Yeah, I was kidding." I actually admired Billy's ability to hook things up. I just didn't share his enthusiasm for the activity. I turned back to Mr. Sinclair. "When does practice start?"

"Next Monday."

Well, whether or not he had any experience as a coach, at least we'd have a team. And I'd get my chance to fence.

The rest of the week and through the weekend, I did all I could to help speed the passage of time toward Monday afternoon. Finally, on Monday, as the school day ended, I hurried to the locker room.

"Holy crap!" I stepped into my worst nightmare—times ten. Every wrestler and basketball player in the school was there, shouting, laughing, snapping towels, torturing small animals. Okay, maybe they weren't all bad guys. There were some casual friends and nodding acquaintances scattered through the mob. But there were also some of the nastiest creatures this side of a Wes Craven film.

I slipped along the side wall and snuck over to my locker, hoping to avoid setting off the victim detectors. If I was quiet enough, the wrestlers would leave me alone.

"Time to fence!"

Billy, grinning like a game-show contestant who'd just won a lifetime supply of matching luggage, rushed over and waved something white up and down in one hand.

"Look, Scott, I got fencing pants. Cool, huh? My mom bought them for me. She's real happy. I'm the first one in our family to go out for a sport." He flapped the white pants in my face like a matador trying to goad a bull.

"Ssshhhh . . ." I said. "This isn't the best time for show-and-tell."

Too late. A passing hand shot between us and snatched Billy's fencing pants. "Check this out," Trent said. "A fag costume."

Billy reached for the pants.

Trent danced backwards. "You know what? You don't need to wear these. You already look like a fag." He glanced around the locker room. I could see his weaselly little brain working out the best way to humiliate Billy. He settled for tossing the pants into the shower where they landed in the middle of the wet, soapy floor.

Billy ran off to retrieve his pants. By the time he returned, Danny had shown up, carrying a pair of sneakers and a sweatsuit. "I don't know about this," he said.

"I don't either." I sighed and tried to hold on to the image I'd started with—me as a cool guy with mask and sword, fencing away while the clash of steel against steel rang through the air. It wasn't easy.

We left the locker room and headed for the girl's gym. Yup—one more indignity. The basketball players got the boy's gym, the swimmers got the pool at the YMCA, the wrestlers got the exercise room, and we got stuck sharing the floor with the clog dancing club.

"Okay, team, line up," Mr. Sinclair called.

"Where are the swords?" Danny whispered as he took a spot to my left.

"Beats me." I looked around for equipment. Not a sword or mask in sight. If the Huns attacked right now, we'd be doomed.

"Hey, Mr. Sinclair! Mr. Sinclair!" Billy shouted, waving his hand.

"Yes?" Mr. Sinclair asked.

"What about our swords? When do we get our swords? Can we get them now? They're the electronic ones, right? When do we get them?"

"After we get in shape," he said. "First, we exercise the body. All together, now. Let's start with jumping jacks." He leaped and clapped. "One, two . . ."

". . . ninety-nine, one hundred."

Oh, man. For the next hour, we exercised. Push-ups. Sit-ups. Throw-ups. Okay, just one of those. But at least it wasn't me rushing off to do a shallow dive into the garbage can.

"Great sport," Danny said as we collapsed on the floor after practice. "I feel so dashing. So honorable. Just kill me now, all right? I don't want to live to see how much my muscles are going to hurt tomorrow."

"I'd kill you if I could lift my hand," I told him. "Maybe next week." I was wiped out. Around me, a quivering assortment of fencers lay in various degrees of trauma.

Through lenses of sweat drops, I watched Mr. Sinclair leave the gym. A moment later, he came rushing back. "I almost forgot—we must jog. It builds stamina." He clapped his hands together. "Everyone up. Come on. Just two laps around the halls. Hurry. All together. Run like a team."

With grunts and groans, the dead rose. Somehow, we

huffed through the empty hallways, completing two circuits around the outer corridor. As we ran, Danny glared at me and muttered, "Yeah, definitely a great sport."

I didn't have enough air in me for a reply. The slap of my sneaker bottoms echoed from the floor to the walls, then took up residence in my head as a mocking chant: *you fool, you fool, you fool* . . . I remember a Stephen King story where kids were forced to keep walking. The ones who stopped got shot. This was worse. We did pretty much the same workout on Tuesday. And Wednesday. And the rest of the first week. There was one advantage to the grueling training. By the middle of the second week, I noticed that gym class didn't seem all that rough. Compared to Mr. Sinclair's routine, Mr. Cadutto's warm-up calisthenics were a joke.

Danny was getting into shape, too. Even Billy and the rest of the team were actually starting to look less like cast members for a low-budget zombie movie. All we now needed was cold steel.

Finally, a week and a half before our first meet, we entered the girl's gym to a lovely sight—stacks of equipment. There was a frenzied rush to the table while Mr. Sinclair pleaded for restraint. I knew what I wanted. I grabbed a saber, the only sword where you could score with the edge of the blade. Sure, the purest fencing was done with the foil, and the épée was challenging, but those swords just used the tip.

The saber I picked was pretty well beaten up. The hand guard was all scratched. That didn't matter. I was happy to have a sword of my own. I stepped away from the mob and sliced the air.

Danny took a saber, too. So did Mike Gottlieb, one of the older kids. "Good choice," he said. "I fenced saber last year."

"Line up," Mr. Sinclair called.

We formed a line, swords in hand. Finally, a chance to cross steel with a worthy opponent. I couldn't wait.

"Swords down," Mr. Sinclair called. "Time for calisthenics."

We put our swords down and exercised. But, halfway through the practice, we got our chance.

"Swords up," Mr. Sinclair called.

"At last," Billy said.

I picked up my saber, eager to cross steel with anyone who dared face me.

"Advance!" Mr. Sinclair called.

We stepped forward.

"Retreat!" he said.

We stepped back.

For the rest of the period, that's what we did. Step forward. Step back. Step forward. Step back. Again and again. Occasionally, for variety, we'd move two steps forward, then two steps back. It's less exciting than it sounds. Far less.

When I got home, I dug through the boxes in the garage until I found Dad's chrome polish. I shined up my sword, then fenced imaginary enemies up and down the hall until Mom yelled at me to stop all that thumping and shouting.

Mr. Sinclair did his best to teach us. He brought in some fencing books from the library. And he talked a coach over at the college into coming by a couple times. The guys who'd fenced last year helped us out, too. Even so, we were pretty bad.

I found out how bad at our opening match. It was an away game against Mercer High. Nine kids fence for a team—three each at foil, saber, and épée. In a match, you get to fence three bouts, going against the guys on the other team with the same weapon as yours.

The meet was in their cafeteria. The tables and chairs had been pushed back to make room for the long mat we fenced on. Wires ran from the scoring machine to reels at each end of the mat.

My first bout, the moment I plugged the cord from

the reel into my saber's handle and slipped on my mask, I forgot absolutely everything I'd learned.

"Fence!" the referee shouted.

Flick. My opponent extended his arm.

Snap. Something hit the side of my mask. Crap. It was the other guy's sword.

One to nothing.

"Fence!"

Flick.

Snap.

Crap.

Two, nothing.

"Fence!"

Flick.

I got smart. I raised my sword, blocking the cut. I blocked air. Tap. He'd switched to a thrust. I looked down at the point where it rested against my chest. Crap.

Three, nothing.

And so it went. Flick, snap, crap. Flick, tap, crap. I lost five, zip.

"Try moving a bit more," Mike said when I walked back to our bench.

"Thanks."

My second bout went better. I lost five nothing again, but it took the other guy longer to win.

"It's okay to use your sword," Danny said.

My third bout, down two, nothing, I started to see the attacks coming. As my opponent made a cut toward my left side, I blocked and counterattacked—a parry and riposte. I think I was as startled as he was when the light went on showing I'd scored.

He scored twice more. But at four to one, I made a fast lunge, catching him as he was coming in and scoring my second point.

I lost the bout. And we lost the match twenty-five to two. It almost didn't matter. I'd fenced. And I'd scored a couple points. That was good enough for now.

As we headed to the parking lot after the match, I

noticed that Mike was grinning like we'd won. "What's so funny?" I asked, following him to the back of the bus.

He opened his coat. A stack of sword blades clattered to the seat.

"Where'd those come from?" I asked.

"Where do you think?" Mike asked.

"You stole them?"

"Sure. It's traditional. The other teams try to steal from us, so we have to steal back. Don't blame me. It's their fault for not keeping an eye on their equipment table."

Ed Drake, the team captain, joined us and added a couple fencing gloves to the pile. Someone else pulled a mask out of his bag.

I couldn't believe it. This was so wrong. Fencing was supposed to be all about rules and honor. I wanted to say something, but I knew it wouldn't make a difference. I took a seat and kept my mouth shut.

We lost our next match, too. This time it was twenty-two to five. It was a home game. Not that it mattered. Nobody came to watch. I lost all three bouts again, but I scored points in each of them.

"Look on the bright side," Danny said as the other team left the gym.

"What's that?" I asked.

"You don't have to use that crappy old scratched-up saber any longer." He pulled a brand-new shiny hand guard from his bag. "Put your blade in this."

"Not you, too," I said.

Danny shrugged. "It all works out. We steal from them. They steal from us."

"Not me." I turned away from him.

"Come on. Lighten up." Danny chased after me. "You aren't angry, are you?"

"No." I was disappointed. But he wouldn't understand. I didn't think anybody understood.

Everyone laughed whenever they heard the fencing

results over morning announcements. The whole school knew I was on the team—thanks to my first day of gym class. I felt like the poster boy for chronic losers. It got even worse when they started reading the individual records.

"And Scott Tarbell now has eighteen losses for the season."

Angelica Carter, who sat to my right, glanced at me and said "They didn't tell us your wins. Shouldn't they mention them, too?"

I just shrugged and tried to look puzzled. After months of searching for a way to impress her, this didn't seem like my best opening.

Halfway through the season, our luck changed. All three of our foil fencers started winning most of their bouts. It wasn't enough to win any of the meets, but it made the team feel better. Then, on our next to last meet, we pulled ahead early. The three guys fencing foils were doing an excellent job. I lost my first bout but won the second. It was only my fifth win for the season. The épées were doing well, too.

But I noticed Ed and Mike exchanging that same grin I'd seen on the bus. Something was up. The other team's coach complained to the referee. They all came over and started to examine the foils.

I knew what they were looking for. When you score a point, it completes a circuit and lights a bulb on the scoring machine. I'd heard rumors of kids trying to rig their swords. I'd even heard a story about a kid who'd tried to short out his foil with a penny. They say it fell out of his hand during the match.

"Nobody'll find anything," Mike whispered to Ed.

"Bridge is a genius," Ed whispered back.

"Is there anything to find?" I asked.

Mike grinned and shrugged. I knew something was going on. But he was right—the referee didn't find anything in the sword. Just to be sure, he made our fencer switch swords. Our guy lost.

The match continued. The score was tied when I came up for the final bout. The moment the match started, I shot out a cut to the head, just to see how my opponent reacted. Much to my surprise, my saber whacked his mask with a satisfying smack. I had an easy point.

I tried it again. Bad move. He lunged under my strike and scored. I faked another head strike. As he lifted his blade to block, I brought my sword around and scored against his right side.

Two to one.

He scored again. Then I scored twice. Four to two. I was almost there.

I stood, ready. I had the advantage. I had the momentum. But we'd cheated. That must have been what Mike and Ed were talking about. I thought about who'd been winning. Ed at first foil, Walter at second foil, and Billy. Oh, man—Billy Esterbridge. Ed had said, "Bridge is a genius." Billy was a hardware geek. If anyone could rig the swords, it was him.

My opponent attacked, jerking me out of my thoughts as his blade smacked my left shoulder.

Four to three.

He came in hard and fast this time. I parried, but I didn't return the attack. I knew I could score, winning the match and the meet. Just like that, I could be the hero. He attacked twice more with the point, and then with a cut. Another attack with the point. I noticed that he always twisted his wrist slightly just before lunging.

No matter how good you are, you can't block forever. On his next attack, his blade nicked my arm just beneath my guard.

Four all.

We faced each other for the final point. I realized I had to make a quick decision. Which was worse—winning a match when my teammates had cheated or letting myself lose a match I was sure I could win?

He turned his wrist slightly. I knew what was coming. He lunged.

I parried the thrust and flicked my blade across the side of his mask.

The team went crazy.

Feeling nothing at all like a hero, I walked through a sea of congratulations and gathered up my stuff. Most of my stuff, that is. Someone had stolen my spare blade from my bag.

As we headed to the locker room, Danny said, "You almost looked like you didn't want to win."

I told him what happened.

"So why'd you score that last point?"

"If I let myself lose, that would be like cheating. Right? Besides, for all I knew, the other team was cheating, too. Maybe every team we ever faced cheated."

"Get over it," Danny said. "There's no honor in the world. This is just a high school sport. It's only cheating if they catch you."

There was no point arguing. I showered and got dressed. Billy came over while I waited for Danny.

"That was great match," he said. "Really great. I'm glad we finally won one."

"Yeah," I said. "Really great."

From behind me came a jeering mocking taunt. "Hey, it's the *girls*."

Oh, crap. Not now. Trent strutted up on his way out of the shower, a towel around his waist and a mocking leer on his face. "I'll bet you guys play with each others swords in the dark." He reached out, grabbing Billy's foil from the bench.

"That's mine," Billy said. "Give it back."

"I'll give it," Trent said. He poked Billy. "You like that? I'll bet you do."

Other wrestlers crowded around, laughing. "Stick him, Trent," someone shouted.

"Shish kebab time."

"Bend over, Billy."

"Cut a Z on him, man."

"No, make it a T for Trent."

I backed away.

Goaded by the laughs, Trent poked Billy again. Harder this time.

"Cut it out," Billy said.

Bad choice of words.

"Cut? Sure, if you want me to." Trent slashed the sword, leaving a long red mark across Billy's chest. He slashed a second time, downward, making a crude T. One small drop of blood oozed from the welt.

"Stop it, shithead!"

Trent snapped around to face me. I don't know which of us was more surprised by my shout.

"What was that?" he asked. "You defending your lover boy?"

Why did it always come to that? I didn't even like Billy. But I had to try to keep him from getting hurt any worse. "Hey—it's not even fair. You have a sword. He doesn't."

"Yeah, *he* doesn't. But *you* do," Trent said. He poked me with the foil. I barely felt it through my winter jacket.

"Just stop it, okay?"

"No. I want to sword fight with you," Trent said. "Come on." He poked me again. I looked at him, standing there in nothing but a towel. I had a heavy jacket. And gloves. It was about as unfair as it could get. I glanced back over at Billy as he sniffled.

"Let's go," Trent said, giving me a third poke.

I reached down to the bench next to me and grabbed my fencing mask. "Okay," I said as I slipped the mask over my head, "let's fence." I pulled my saber from my bag.

Trent laughed as I got into position. To the untrained eye, the fencing stance probably looks wimpy. Actually, it looks pretty wimpy to the trained eye, too. But it works.

Trent let out a yell and slashed at me like some sort

of malfunctioning Audioanimatronic from a Disney ride.

I parried his attack effortlessly. After a match where I'd faced three experienced fencers, this was a joke. He slashed again. This time, I followed my parry with a move of my own, flicking the blade across Trent's shoulder.

"Ouch," he yelped, taking a step backwards.

I pressed forward, easily blocking each of his clumsy slashes, and easily picking away at him. Even with the blunted tip and dulled blade, a saber can hurt—especially against bare flesh.

It wasn't fair. Not at all. I was heavily protected, and heavily skilled compared to my opponent. Trent had a sword he didn't know how to use and a towel. He had no more chance of beating me at fencing than I did of beating him at wrestling. It wasn't fair at all. It violated everything I'd ever believed about fair play and honor.

But it sure felt right.

With each thrust, I forced him farther back. The crowd of wrestlers moved with us, keeping clear of our blades, but following right behind as we passed the last row of lockers and reached the end of the corridor.

I halfway expected one of Trent's friends to clobber me from behind. But nobody interfered.

As Trent put his back against the locker room door, I charged, giving him a stinging assault on both arms. Then I thrust my point toward his face. I was only faking, but Trent didn't know that.

He howled and stumbled backwards—right into the hall. I followed, leaping through the doorway. I had him moving now. Halfway down the hall, I did something I never could have done to a real fencer.

I disarmed him.

It was so slick. I caught the middle of his blade with my tip, spun my wrist, and sent his sword into the air. If only Angelica Carter had been there to see that move. Without a doubt, it was the coolest thing I'd ever done.

I even caught the falling sword in my left hand. As I

stood holding both swords, a dozen movies flashed through my mind. All my heroes would do the same thing now. They'd bow and return the weapon, rearming their opponent. Then they'd smile and say, "Shall we continue?" That was the honorable thing. That was fair play.

"The hell with that," I said.

This wasn't a movie. This was high school. I lunged with both swords and buried the tips in the towel. With a yank, I pulled the towel from Trent and flicked it over my shoulder.

Weaponless and naked, Trent turned and ran, vanishing around the corner. I didn't follow.

I pivoted and found myself facing the rest of the wrestling team. Even with two swords, I felt badly unequipped.

Bruno Haskins smacked me on the shoulder. "Pretty cool," he said. "You're good with that sword, man."

"Did you see that jerk go running?" another wrestler said.

Bruno laughed and shook his head. "Trent is such an idiot." He walked off with his friends, who trailed their thoughts behind them.

"Freakin' moron . . ."

". . . what a loser . . ."

"You see him run?"

"Total jerk . . ."

The distant sound of female screams told me Trent had been spotted. I found Billy and returned his sword, then grabbed my bag. "Wow. One for all and all for one," Billy said.

"Right." I didn't shatter his illusion that he'd participated. He needed his dreams, too.

"Those guys could have killed you," Danny said as we headed out.

"Yeah. I know."

He shrugged. "I guess they didn't really like Trent, either."

"Maybe there's some hope for them, after all." I took off my mask and looked at my sword. In the dented hand guard, my reflection was oddly contorted. But there was no hiding the smile. I wasn't Zorro. And I wasn't John Steed or Captain Blood. But I was a fencer. That was good enough for me.

We lost our last match. Badly. Mr. Sinclair insisted on inspecting all the swords himself. Whatever way Billy had rigged the electronics, Mr. Sinclair was a good enough physics teacher to figure it out. It didn't matter. Win or lose, I loved fencing. Even if marked me as a dork.

After all that, I wasn't even able to go out for tennis. Someone ratted on me, and I got handed thirty days' detention. I guess that was fair enough. I'd happily have given sixty days in exchange for that one moment. In a perfect world, my victory over Trent would have earned the guys on the fencing team at least a bit of respect. But the glamour didn't last. We went back to being the butt of jokes pretty quickly. On the other hand, nobody ever touched our swords again.

The Book

Shelley Stoehr

Recently, when my parents were cleaning out the eaves next to my old bedroom, they discovered a secret hiding place of mine, and some old letters I'd written in high school hidden under a floorboard. Receiving those letters, still tied up neatly with string to show my parents hadn't read them, was the inspiration for my story "The Book."

As I reread those letters, I remembered how serious my teenaged secrets seemed to me back then. In fact, both the letters and the heartbreak that inspired them were very innocent, and not so life-changing or earth-shattering as I'd believed back when I'd written them. But I wondered, as I recalled those days, what if there'd been a *real* secret—a big, terrible, crushing secret hidden under those floorboards? My imagination started spinning into gear. . . . Better yet, I thought, what if the real secret was tucked away in the shadows of the protagonist's own mind, purposely forgotten, until finding some old letters and a notebook gradually made her remember . . .

There really was a "Book of Michael Cortese," and a boy by that name with whom I was utterly obsessed in high school. I've used his real name in this story because I couldn't imagine replacing it. The song "Hotdogs and Pekingese" was also real, though different girl, different situation. The rest of the story is—thankfully—fiction.

At the time I thought it was love. Even years of therapy couldn't convince me otherwise. It was finding "The Book of Michael Cortese" that convinced me my relationships with boys had always been more obsession than love. I still didn't want to believe it, but there it was, dusty and yellowing, one corner chewed off by mice, right in front of me.

I found "The Book of Michael Cortese" under a floorboard in the eaves next to my old bedroom in my parents' house. My secret hiding place—when I was little, I used to drag a blanket and a lamp into the eaves late at night, to read after lights-out. Later, I sneaked into the dusty, dark crawlspace to smoke cigarettes—in fact, there was half a pack under the floorboard too, right under The Book. Also there, carefully tied together with string, were letters I'd never sent, where I'd poured my teenaged heart out in secret. I remembered retreating to the eaves to write them, where no one would see me crying. They would've laughed at me. They wouldn't have believed I was in love. They might've said that I was obsessed with those boys.

The letters, like the eaves themselves, brought back memories of years of boys I'd loved, beginning with Michael Harris in fourth-through-sixth grades—my very first love—through Michael Lutz in seventh, and ending with Michael Cortese, grades eight-to-ten for me, ten-to-twelve for him. He was my last Michael, and the last of my obsessions to be hidden under the floorboard in the eaves. I wish I could say it was because I stopped crying over boys in the dark after I grew up, but it was only that I stopped writing love letters after the accident. I continued my obsessive relationships—there was Gary, then Jeff, then Steven and Dale—but only one *Book*. Finding it made me realize that I hadn't been in love with any of those boys—probably not even Michael.

Pulling a cigarette from the stale, half pack, I lit it, watching dust from the eaves swirl with the smoke, and waiting for the tears to come. They boiled inside me, but wouldn't come out. Running my finger over the dusty cover of "The Book of Michael Cortese," I smiled at the little hearts I'd used to dot the *i*'s in Michael.

God, it still hurts. Like it was yesterday.

Opening The Book was like opening a wound. Every page was a layer of skin that had grown over painful memories from high school—especially the one, the big one, which I wasn't ready to remember yet. I concentrated on The Book instead.

Funny, how it had started out as a plain spiral-bound notebook. Inside the front cover was a heart with "M. C. + J. B. Forever" scrawled inside it that I remembered drawing. I remembered the day I tore out the Social Studies notes from the beginning of the notebook, and made it my Bible.

It was the last school day before Christmas vacation. I was in eighth grade, and Michael was in tenth. Dashing out of my fifth-period French class, I said "Later" to my best friend Anne before she could stop me to talk, pushing past her and weaving through the kids heading up the stairs, as I struggled to get downstairs in time.

Get out of my way! Move! Move! Move! I screamed in my head, frustrated with the slow-moving, faceless masses. Suddenly I realized I was moving my lips—I hoped I hadn't actually screamed anything out loud. Michael was my secret, and no one could know how much I loved him, or how important it was for me to get to his locker in time.

Looking back, I'm amazed how fast I could move, in spite of my super-tight jeans and the big, dangling earrings that swung and bounced against my head. I got there just in time to see him find the gift Anne and I had slid between the slots at the top of his locker early that morning. I'd painted him a very small watercolor, which had just fit. Michael and I were both artists, which was part of what had drawn me to him in the first place, so I knew he'd like it. Of course, I didn't sign it. I just figured he'd *know* . . .

. . . that I painted the picture, that I was mature for my age, that we were perfect for each other . . .

I followed Michael to our next class—well, his English class, and my Social Studies. But the rooms were next-door to each other, separated only by a sliding partition. I don't know how I made it through Social Studies that year at all, I was so much more focused on the sounds from the other side of the partition than the notes being given in my own room.

"Who Can It Be Now" by Men at Work was playing loudly from next door, annoying the crap out of my Social Studies teacher. Michael's class was having a Christmas party! I wished, and wished, and wished . . . and the door opened! Our class was invited! We could just slide the partition out of the way and . . .

"I don't think so," said my teacher, Mr. Edwards. "And turn down that noise."

My brain burned, as anger like a snake slinked through me, gleaming yellow in the narrowed slits of my eyes, which glistened, trying not to cry—trying to shoot poison instead, and kill Mr. Edwards for keeping me from the love of my life. Slowly, so no one would notice, I began to tear out every page of notes in my Social Studies notebook, one by one. I felt like crumpling them, but there was still a reasonable part of me left inside—presently being choked by the poisonous snake wrapped around my mind, but not quite crushed—which made me keep the torn-out pages, stuffed into another notebook in case I needed them to study later.

When I was done ripping out the notes, I drew a heart inside the front cover, and filled it with dreams. Closing the notebook, I laid my palm over it and turned my head so I could hear the music from beyond the partition better. It calmed me down. I pictured Michael's face, and the snake inside me was charmed into a gently swaying trance.

Sliding another cigarette from the pack I'd found under the floorboard, I flipped slowly through The Book. I'd recorded Michael's address and phone number there, and his class schedule, which Anne and I had spent half a semester figuring out, to make it easier to "accidentally" run into him in the hall between classes . . .

God, how I remembered those mad dashes through the halls, and how worth it it was just to catch a glimpse of him, hoping to catch his eye.

. . . There were line drawings he'd done for the school paper, and pieces of a watercolor he'd started in art class and thrown out. I remembered how I got that—Anne had been serving detention in the art room during his class, and she'd rescued the scraps from the garbage can for me.

Sick, I thought now, as I ran my fingertip over the uneven surface of paper, Michael's discarded dragon painting that I had carefully uncrumpled, and lovingly put back together, smoothing his scraps into my notebook forever.

My God, I was a stalker!

Funny, how ten years later I could still put a time and place and feeling to everything in The Book, even the little things, like a corner of napkin where he'd written "Bite me," that had been passed to me in the cafeteria by accident. Well, at least it seemed like an accident at the time. Back then I never would've imagined Michael wanting me to bug off. It always seemed to me like he was secretly, deeply in love with me, and maybe just didn't know it yet.

Turning another page in The Book, I came to where I'd taped in the bolt he'd thrown at me while we were working together on the set of *Fiddler on the Roof* after school. I remembered, he was painting a backdrop of a dirt road.

I stopped what I was doing to watch Michael, high on the ladder, painting. We were alone, gloriously, miraculously, excitingly alone. I had to make a connection, it was now or never.

He noticed me. "What're you looking at?" he wanted to know, as he climbed down off the ladder.

Guessing what he really meant was "Stop looking at me," I looked down, and didn't see where the bolt came from, or if he was actually throwing it *at* me, or only in my general direction. Anyway, it didn't hit me, just startled me as it bounced and rolled, stopping at my feet. Furtively, I glanced up. He wasn't even looking at me, only at his painting. Pocketing the bolt, I rubbed it between my fingers like a talisman, knowing *he touched it*. Hoping, as only a freak like me would, that *he threw it at me!*

Meanwhile, Michael had climbed back up the ladder, dabbed some darker-brown texture onto the road, and was leaning back to examine the result. He frowned. "It's still not right," he said.

He wants my opinion! Stepping back to the edge of the stage, I cocked my head, trying to figure out the problem. "There's something funny about the road," I said. I really wanted to be helpful.

"Duh," he said. Then, "What're you doing here anyway?"

"You told me to paint this fence."

"So paint the freakin' fence."

"It looks like it's just been stuck on, like it's not going anywhere or something," I said, still squinting at the road.

"Tell me again, why are you here?"

My heart was beating fast. *OhmiGod he's talking to me! He's actually* talking *to me!* "Maybe if you put some bushes along the side of the road it would help," I suggested.

"You want bushes? I'll give you some freakin' bushes," Michael said, not so much in a mean or aggravated way as in a playful, friendly way, I thought, as I watched him dab on puffs of forest green alongside the edges of the road.

"There's your freakin' bushes," he said when he was done. "You happy now?"

He wants to know if I'm happy! I thought, rubbing the bolt in my pocket. As he leaned back to look at his work again, I did the same, tilting my head and squinting like before. The bushes helped, but didn't really fix the road. Something was off with the perspective. . . .

But I answered, "It looks better," and went back to what I was supposed to be doing—painting the fence brown, and stealing glances at Michael, high above me on the ladder, trying to make the road right.

I bought a yearbook Michael's senior year. Sitting in the eaves of my parents' house ten years later, wiping dirty tears from my cheeks and coughing from stale cigarette smoke, I wondered what happened to it. I remembered I scratched out Becky Weiss's face in every one of her pictures. Although she was a major part of Michael's life for almost a year, she didn't appear in "The Book of Michael Cortese" at all. I had a picture from the school paper, of Michael as "Felix" in the senior play, *The Odd Couple*. Becky played one of the Pigeon sisters. There was a Becky-shaped hole cut out of the picture I'd glued into The Book, followed by a song Anne and I had made up about her hairy knees.

The song was silly and pointless, and it made me laugh in spite of myself, which was a relief, and a surprise, considering how I'd felt about Becky when I was in tenth grade. Although looking back, I don't think I hated her so much as I only wanted to *be* her.

Technically, there were two cast parties—one for the seniors, and one for the rest of the Drama Club, underlings like Anne and I who only painted sets and stuff.

But Anne's brother was friends with the guy throwing the party, so we got to go anyway. First thing I wanted to do when we got there was find Michael. Anne rolled her eyes, and for a second I was sorry I ever told her about Michael Cortese. Making tight fists with my hands, I stuffed them into the pockets of my jeans. Anne wouldn't see me cry.

Quietly walking away from my friend, holding my feelings in, I slipped through the seniors partying in the living room without anyone even noticing I was there. Depeche Mode was playing on the stereo, blasting "Your Own Personal Jesus," while I scanned the couches and corners for Michael. He wasn't there, and for a moment I felt almost crippled by the weight of my disappointment.

Outside on the patio the night was hot. My new bra itched. I was afraid if I wiped the sweat on my face, my makeup would smear. My jeans stuck to my legs like dark-blue skin.

"Hey, look what I found in the kitchen," said Anne, suddenly appearing out of the shadows of seniors dancing. She handed me a red plastic cup filled with foul-smelling purple liquid.

Sipping carefully, I almost spit it out. "What *is* it?" I whispered, so none of the older kids would hear.

"I made it," she whispered back. "Vodka, tequila, peach schnapps, and grape juice. It's good, huh?"

I shrugged. Taking another sip, I thought, *Well, it's not* that *bad. Maybe it'll make me less nervous.*

"Hey, it's like way hot out here!" said Anne, following me as I wove through the patio furniture, trying not to stare at the couples making out, but having to *look*, to see if Michael was there. Gulping at the purple drink now, I disappeared into a fantasy, letting it appear in my mind's eye like it was real . . .

Michael all alone on a chaise longue, and me just casually sitting next to him, telling how I felt. Him reach-

ing out and stroking my cheek with his hand. Saying he was glad I found him.

The fantasy changed—I had a million of them back then.

Becky on a chaise with another guy, and Michael freaking out when he saw, and me being there to comfort him. Him kissing me.

As I slinked through the seniors in the yard, searching for Michael, sipping my drink, and sweating from the heat, I peeked back at the patio doors.

Michael, drunk, falling through the glass, and me rushing to hold his head, using what I'd learned in first aid to save him.

Then I had the same fantasy the other way around, where he saved me.

Anne pulled my ear. "Hey, are you in there?" she wanted to know. "I said it's too hot out here, let's go back inside. Wanna 'nother drink?" she continued when she had my attention.

Well, since Michael's not here, I thought. "I guess so," I said, letting her pull my arm, leading me back. As we crossed the patio, I noticed a group playing Quarters at one of the tables, the citronella candles casting strange shadows on their laughing faces.

The house going up in flames, and me rushing back in to get Michael from where he was trapped in the bathroom, and then dragging him out to safety.

Him dragging me out of the burning house.

Him tasting my drink and liking it. Me offering to make him another one.

Him asking if I wanna take a ride on his motorcycle.

Driving all night without our helmets, the wind rushing through his hair, blowing it into my face . . . the softness, and sweet salty smell of it . . .

. . . Michael and Becky cuddled up on the couch, doing body shots of tequila. He had a lime between his teeth. She sprinkled salt on his neck, licked it off, and slammed back a shot. I turned away before she started sucking the lime.

Following Anne into the kitchen, I said, "Don't make me another drink. Let's just do shots."

"I don't know," she said. "I have to drive."

"Fine then," I said, taking some of my anger out on Anne. It was like a snake was wrapped around my throat, choking me. I barely got the words out—"I'll do 'em by myself then."

Anne stared at me as I poured tequila into the bottom of my cup, dumped salt on the back of my hand, licked it and drank. There were no limes in the kitchen. *Damn!* It almost made me cry. All I wanted was what Becky had.

"How was it?" Anne wanted to know. "Was it really gross?"

I shrugged, feeling the warmth burn up the angry snake inside. "No, it's not that bad," I said, pouring another shot.

"Do you feel drunk?"

I poked my arm—it felt normal. I looked around—nothing was blurred or swaying, only tainted by the vision of Michael and Becky together on the couch. Other than the dead weight of unrequited love pulling me down, I felt fine.

I shrugged, and Anne grabbed the tequila. "Okay, but only one," she said. She drank it straight from the bottle.

Someone was calling me from downstairs. Taking "The Book of Michael Cortese" with me, I crawled out of the eaves. I heard the call again. It was my husband, John.

"Jesse? Everything okay up there?"

"Yeah," I answered. "I'll be right down."

"Anything I can do?"

Just hearing his voice made me smile, in spite of the memories rushing back at me. It was nice to have someone obsessed with *me* for a change. *No, it wasn't obsession. It was love.*

"I'm okay," I called out as I pulled myself up off the floor, using the dresser for support. I felt dirty, and not just from the gray layer of dust that had settled over me while I was in the eaves. I wished we hadn't come today. If I hadn't been cleaning out my old room, I wouldn't have found The Book, and the past could've stayed buried.

My braces were leaning against the windowsill. As I edged toward them, I could see the house where the Gertzes used to live.

God, I was so mad at her!

She just kept poking me in the arm, until finally I turned and snapped, "All right already! *What do you want?*"

Becky was in the bathroom puking, and somehow I'd maneuvered myself onto the couch next to Michael. When I yelled at Anne, he looked at me, and my whole face got hot with embarrassment. I glared at my friend.

"Jesse, we have to *go*!" she said.

"Not now," I whispered, looking back at Michael. He was swaying a little—I wasn't sure if it was him, or me. We'd both had a lot of tequila.

Anne was still poking me. "Jesse, I'm smeeri . . . I mean, I'm *seri*ous!" she said, pushing herself up off the floor and using the arm of the couch to pull herself the rest of the way up. "We were supposed to be home at twelf . . . twel . . . midnight. My father's gonna kill me."

"But . . ."

"But he's gonna kill me, Jesse!"

"You go ahead then, I'll get another ride," I said, peeking at Michael out of the corner of my eye, remembering the fantasy—*me and him on his motorcycle, riding until sunrise, the wind rushing through . . .*

"Becky's gonna be back in a sec . . . second," Anne

managed to say, even though she was beginning to hiccup.

As if those were the magic words, I did see Becky, emerging carefully from the hallway behind Anne, kind of wobbly, but definitely capable of making it to the couch. I stood up quickly, before the ultimate embarrassment of having to be asked to move.

Thanks a lot, I thought at Anne as we stepped over bodies and weaved through dancers. *The whole night is ruined, and it's all your fault,* I thought as she searched through her purse for the keys to her father's car.

"Just a second, I'll be right back," I said.

"Jesse!" she whined.

"I said I'll be one second!"

Hurrying back to the living room, I just had to see if Becky had landed on the couch. I had to know what Michael was doing.

He was holding her head in his lap, stroking her hair. God! I wanted to kill her! Instead, I grabbed the bottle of tequila and her shot glass, poured one, and tossed it back. The burn in my throat was nothing compared to the burn in my mind, but it was all numbed when Michael suddenly smiled at me, giving me a thumbs-up. My heart skipped a beat. Turning quickly away so he wouldn't see me blush, I ran back to where Anne was waiting by the front door. I could hardly feel the floor under my feet, I was so excited. *He smiled at me!*

Lightweights, I thought as I weaved through the few remaining dancers and stepped over the many fallen bodies again. *I'm not even drunk, and they're* seniors. I felt like I was way more mature than any of them, and when Michael smiled at me it was because he realized it too.

"OhmiGod, wait 'til I tell you what just happened . . ." I began as we headed out into the night, toward Anne's father's car.

* * *

I didn't hear John come into the room behind me as I stared out the window in my old bedroom, remembering that night. When he touched me, I was so startled, I almost fell. He caught me with both arms around my waist.

Kissing my neck gently, he asked, "Finished yet? Your mom made lunch." He reached for my braces, helping me fasten them to my arms.

> "Hot dogs and Pekingese,
> Becky has hairy knees,
> and she is such a tease,
> hot dogs and Pekingese.
> Hot dogs and Pekingese,
> beware of Becky, please—"

I was singing the song Anne and I wrote the summer before, between turns on the diving board. I interrupted myself to ask, "—So what do you think it meant when Michael smiled at me?"

We were approaching the light at Main Street. Anne shrugged as she turned to look at me, making the car swerve pretty dramatically.

"Whoa! Hey! Are you sure you're okay to drive?" I asked as I grabbed for the steering wheel. We narrowly missed smashing into the rear of a parked car.

"I better slow down," Anne agreed, although all she did was press the gas a little harder. Then she took up singing the song where I left off.

> ". . . or she will give you fleas,
> hot dogs and Pekingese.
> Hot dogs and—"

"—Red light! Red light! Stop! *Red!*" I screamed, grabbing the wheel at the same time, which probably made it worse. After that I remember tires squealing, and the smell of rubber burning as Anne slammed on the brakes, sending us into a spin right in the middle of the Main Street intersection. The car stalled out, and I was shouting, "Do something! Do something!"

"What? What do I do?" Anne screamed back at me, pounding the gas and brakes both at the same time with her feet while I pulled on the steering wheel, trying to make it move. We didn't even see the other car coming, turning the corner from Dear Park Avenue too fast, slamming into my side and crushing one of my legs. We plowed into a streetlight, which was driven into Anne's side of the car, pinning her in an unnatural position as her window was smashed in. What I remember most was the large triangle of glass sticking out of Anne's neck like something in a cartoon—it seemed so *big*, bigger than the window had been, *huge*, and there was blood everywhere, more blood than I'd ever seen, even on TV.

"Hey, what's this?" John asked, picking up "The Book of Michael Cortese" where I'd dropped it.

I barely heard him. "I think the Gertzes moved away because they couldn't stand to look at me. They never blamed me though," I said to myself, turning away from the window, and looking at John for forgiveness, because it was too late to ask for Anne's.

"Huh?" said John, still flipping through the book, not looking up. He was smiling, almost laughing. " 'Hot dogs and Pekingese'? What does that mean? Sing it for me, Jesse, I have to hear it! Hey, where's 'The Book of John Elferrs'? Where's *my* Book?" He started toward the eaves.

"Don't!" I said, too sharply. Then I added, softly, "I mean, let's just go have lunch." I turned away, so he wouldn't see the tears streaking through the dirt on my face.

"What do you want to do with this?" he wanted to know, meaning The Book.

"Throw it out," I said at first. Then I stopped. "No, wait," I said. Turning on my good leg, I looked up at my husband sadly, letting him see me cry for the first time.

"Are you okay?" John asked, hurrying to my side as I sat on the edge of the bed.

I took The Book from him, and then just held it at first, afraid. When I finally opened it, it looked different. It wasn't "The Book of Michael Cortese" anymore, it was "The Book of Jesse Blaise and Anne Gertz." For the first time since she died, I wanted to talk about her. She'd been my best friend. She'd been there, through so many of my first loves, and especially through my obsession with Michael Cortese—and she'd never laughed at me.

After the accident, no one ever blamed me, but I did. I knew the whole story. I'd just forgotten it until now, when finding The Book brought it all back, all the secrets I'd buried under the floorboard in the eaves.

"Do you want to talk about it?" John asked, as if he read my mind.

"Yeah, I think I should," I said. It was time to finally stop crying alone in the dark. It was time to grow up.

To Express How Much

Mary Ann McGuigan

"To Express How Much" is about revealing your secret self and risking rejection. We have good reason to be wary of sharing our feelings. People can hurt and betray us. But hiding has its costs.

When I was very young, I used writing to create a place where grownups couldn't go. Life with my family was tumultuous, often violent, and always seemingly one step away from financial and emotional disaster. Into my stories I put my fears, hopes, shame, and wishes for what life could be. Those stories and nearly all of what I wrote until *Cloud Dancer* was published in 1994 remained a secret.

In high school, I first met others who wrote fiction. I shared stories, but never the ones about growing up the way I had and the lingering challenge of sorting it all out. It was not until I was grown up with two children of my own that I began to share such stories with other writers and submit them for publication. I saw in the responses to my writing that it touched the hiding places in people—even those who'd grown up under very different, more fortunate circumstances.

The scariest risk came when I chose to stop hiding—even under the cover of fiction—who I was and how I had grown up. In return has come lasting friendship.

Grown-ups often look back and wish they'd done things differently. I suppose "To Express How Much" is my way of doing that and of wishing too that I might keep at least one young person from waiting as long as I did.

Jack read the last lines of his story, folded it and shifted in his chair, not yet ready to look at our faces. He'd written about an eighteen-year-old who leaves his family behind in Milwaukee and sets out across the country. We laughed at how the kid wakes up under a broad, distinguished tree and slowly realizes that he's crawling with spiders who've been tasting his freckles all night. But later at the end, when the character winds up sitting next to an old man on a bus, comparing how alone and scared they are, Jack got the feelings just right. I'd never heard another guy talk about things like that before.

"That's your best so far, Jack," Karen said. Karen tended to speak only in superlatives, but I thought so too.

"It is," someone agreed. Melanie was crying. Melanie cried every time a story showed that life could be less than kind. She wrote mostly poetry about regrets and destiny that was generally not to my liking, but every now and then she'd come up with an image that would capture a feeling so perfectly it had the impact of a double play in a tight game.

We talked about Jack's story for a long while, telling him what we thought worked, what didn't, until we wandered into talking about what life could be like on our own, away from the choices adults made for us. I could see the subject was making Beth uncomfortable. She kept checking her watch.

Finally she stood and said it was time to go. "Your house next week, Mike, right?" Beth said. She sounded determined, suspicious that I might try to get out of it again. I wanted to, but I'd run out of excuses. The next meeting would have to be at my house. We'd started the group eight weeks before, six of us from Mrs. Irving's Creative Writing class. There were three other juniors, two seniors and me. We wanted a chance to read the stuff that was too personal or too important to share in class.

Everyone had agreed that we'd take turns meeting at each other's houses. My turn had come the sixth week, but I'd said my mother had the flu and we shouldn't risk getting sick. The seventh week I told them the living room was being painted and the place smelled terrible. But the following week it would have to be at my house.

The group met on Tuesday nights at seven o'clock. On my father's good nights, it wouldn't be a problem. He'd be home already and settled into his TV chair, watching game shows until a ball game started. But if he got off early and went out, he would be getting home about seven, and that could mean anything. At the very least a screaming argument with my mother, more likely dishes flying or a lamp smashing. I pictured Jack's face—and Beth's—in the middle of all that. They'd never feel comfortable with me again, even if they had the good manners to keep quiet about it. They'd know then that the stories I shared with them—the ones that were supposed to be as raw and honest as their own—had nothing to do with my real life. But honest or not they were stories, attempts at shaping something of my own. What would be the point of reading them the stories I wrote about the pain I live in?

The group had been Jack's idea. His mother was a real writer, published and everything, and she belonged to a group that talked about what they wrote. So Jack and Beth had started the group off. Somehow, Mrs. Irving had gotten it into her head that I had what it takes, and almost every week she'd set aside my paper to read aloud to the class. I guess that's why Jack and Beth had included me.

Being asked to join the group was the best thing that had happened to me since I came to Jefferson last year. We'd moved again because my father had to start a new job. He'd pissed off his boss and gotten fired. He only said angry things when he was drinking; he didn't mean them. Everybody knew he didn't mean them. But this was my fourth school in eight years. I was an outsider again, and kids felt strange with me. It wasn't that they were unfriendly. I just didn't know what to say to people, how to get beyond polite.

I could only do people on paper. On paper the world became what I wanted it to be. And now that I'd found others who understood what that meant, I had to find a way to keep them.

There was no point in talking to my mother about my father's drinking. She never talked about it. She would just clean up whatever was broken, put it back together if she could. Later, when my father had fallen asleep, I'd hear her crying in her room. At breakfast the next day, you'd swear nothing had happened.

I knew I'd have to talk to my father myself. I waited till Monday night, found him in the garage, working on the car again. I hung around, aimless, spinning the screwdrivers that hung in their neat little niches.

"What's up with you?" he said. He was bent over the engine, his head deep into its parts.

"Nothing," I said.

"Has to be something," he said, his voice muffled behind the raised hood.

"Nothing."

"What?"

I waited until he'd finished tightening something. "Some friends of mine are coming over tomorrow night." I took a few steps toward him, smelled the mixture of grease and gasoline that shrouded him whenever he tended to the car. These smells had always comforted me. They signaled that he was sober, predictable.

"Yeah, so?"

"We have a group," I said, coming closer, leaning against the Buick's passenger side.

"What do you mean a group?"

"A writer's group."

"A what?"

"We read stuff to each other, stuff we've written, and talk about it."

"What kind of stuff?" He was standing upright now, fighting open some stubborn piece of motor with a grimy cloth.

"Different things. Essays, poems, some stories."

"You, too? You still writin' that stuff?"

"Some." When I didn't say any more, he went back into the engine, cursed softly at its insides. "So it's my turn tomorrow night," I said loud enough to be heard over the hood. "To meet here."

He stood again, looked at me longer this time. "So how come you're telling me? Is Mom against this or something?"

"No." I shrugged. "I just thought you'd want to know."

"Okay, so I know," he said, and looked at me, puzzled. "Now are you gonna tell me what this is really about?" I rolled my eyes and moved back to the door to the house. He went back to the engine. I was almost back in the house before I made myself say it.

"Dad." He didn't hear me. "Dad."

"Yeah. What?" He straightened up and looked at me again, annoyed this time.

"I don't want them to see you and Mom fighting." His shoulders slouched and he looked away, as if he'd been accused, exposed. I waited for him to answer. He didn't, and I turned toward the door again, but he called me back.

"Mike, gimme a break," he said. "Who are these friends, anyway? You think their folks don't have disagreements?"

"Disagreements," I mumbled. The word came out with a chuckle that mocked.

"That's right, disagreements," he said, ready for an argument.

"Yeah, they disagree. They just don't bust up the furniture."

My father looked away from me, shook his head as if there had been some grand misunderstanding. He leaned heavily on one arm, stared into the engine without really seeing it. The silence was pretty much what I'd expected. It had taken me so long, so many years, to talk about this with him, to name it. It wasn't his anger that had prevented me; he never gets seriously angry unless he's drunk. I guess I just didn't want to be the one to break the news.

It's ironic how my mother and I protect my father from himself, keep him from having to face who he is and what he does to us. But that's the drill. That's why we all pretend there's nothing wrong.

"The lamp was an accident. You know that." He spoke into the engine, avoiding my eyes.

He was talking about Friday night, the last time he'd come home drunk and crazed. All I said was, "Come on, Dad." I didn't mention the countless other lamps or the tables or the vases or even the toppled Christmas tree one year. But our home isn't just a war zone; it's a prison. We can't let anyone in and we never really get out. The tension gets inside you. You carry it around with you all the time. I was exhausted from it, tired of having to factor his insanity into every part of my life.

"It was just a lamp, for Pete's sake. What do you want from me?"

"My friends are going to be here tomorrow night. I want you to stay sober—for one night. That's what I want."

"Come over here," he said, stepping away from the engine. When I went to him, he talked low, as if what he was telling me needed to be kept just between us. "That don't mean nothing when me and your mother fight. You understand? We're okay. It's nothing to worry about."

"Okay. Sure," I said.

"And don't worry about your friends either. I'll be home early. I'll bring home some chips and we can nuke some popcorn. Think they'd like that?"

"Yeah, sure." He knew he hadn't convinced me, but I didn't have the energy to say anymore.

I felt his callused hand on my arm. "That's not a promise, Mike. That's a fact. Understand?"

I didn't answer, just began walking away. "Hey," he called. "You think I don't know how important this is, this group? You think I don't know what a good writer you are?" He moved toward me, awkward but determined about something. He put the cloth down on the fender of the car, reached into his back pocket for his wallet, pulled a faded, frayed paper out of a secret place. "See this?" he said. "This is that composition you wrote for me for Father's Day." He opened it up, a single folded page, thin and yellowing, precariously delicate. The creases had worn some of the words away. "Jeez, it must have been six years ago. You were only this high. I read this to the guys at work. This was really something. It had Callahan in tears."

I remembered it. I remembered how he laughed at me when my hand trembled as I gave it to him. He called me Shakes for Shakespeare for weeks after. I never knew he'd even read it a second time. "Oh, that thing." I laughed. The composition had been assigned to my whole fifth grade class: "Why I'm So Proud of My Dad." I remember everyone leaning over their papers, gripping their pencils. My paper sat there blank, shouting at me like an accusation. I stared outside. A window near my desk was open and I could see birds moving in and out of trees, hear a lawn mower in the distance, someone calling "David," sounding worried.

I knew what I would write. I'd stay with the safe stuff, talk about how he worked hard and mowed the lawn and fixed the car. I'd make it sound normal. They'd never know the difference. But every word I wrote that day shut out another screaming to be heard. Each one separated me from myself a little more, until the shame I felt about my father became something outside of me, something I didn't have to feel. I was splitting—half lies, half pain—and I knew even then that if I let it happen I'd lose something I'd never get back. That was the night I wrote my first story about what it was really like to be my father's son. He never saw that. No one has. When Father's Day came, I gave him the one I'd been assigned.

We didn't say much for a minute, and then, with great care, he put the paper back into its hidden place in the wallet.

"Don't be worried," he said finally. "Understand?"

"Okay," I said, but I was.

Beth was tapping her pencil to the rhythm of whatever it was dancing in her head. It's a sure thing it had nothing to do with the Stamp Act. Beth could never manage to focus long in Mr. Gleason's class. She'd wind up passing me notes and building tiny paper chairs from the pages of her rainbow-colored assignment pad.

This time I was the first to send mail. I wanted to let her know all systems were go for the group to meet at my house that night. She sent the note back with her typically brief commentary to any news good, bad or neutral. "Okay," she wrote, then followed it with some lines from "A Considerable Speck," a poem by Robert Frost about a mite that lands on his writing paper.

It seemed too tiny to have room for feet,
Yet must have had a set of them complete
To express how much it didn't want to die.

Beth was inviting me, I knew, to take off with it, add some lines of my own. She would go on this way for long whiles, building on whatever you gave her, but in any other communication with me she was brief and guarded, just as she was in her stories. Beth is very pretty, not a studied pretty, but she has a disarming kind of face and manner that really takes you, and I thought when I first met her that she just wanted to discourage me from getting any ideas.

But I realized soon that no one was allowed to get too close to Beth and that in fact she tolerated my company better than most. Beth's was not the welcome ear for tales of how you spent your weekend or complaints about school or parents. She told me once that when people had nothing to worry about they created something instead. I had guessed then that her impatience came from having wealthy parents whose lives were free of anything more difficult than gloomy headlines or a drop in the Dow. She lived in a huge house and had a gardener and a housekeeper. She already had her own car. Her parents, the little I'd seen of them, were beautiful. They looked as if they'd been polished and buffed. There was no question where Beth had gotten her looks, but unlike their daughter, they seemed wooden, as if guessing at how they should behave.

I passed the lines to Beth and watched her smile.

> *I touched the nib to the page, a bridge to higher*
> *spheres, but it scooted round a capital D*
> *and slipped between the lines to find its own escape.*

She bent over the page, eager to respond and pass it back.

> *I watched it wander through the lines,*
> *impervious to where they led,*
> *insisting on its own direction.*

My turn got interrupted by the bell so I scribbled "to be continued" and passed the note back. She smiled and said, "A deal," and I was struck again by how her smile made me feel. It was like a direction, something to head toward.

"Hey," I said, "should I call you?"

She looked at me, puzzled.

"With directions," I said.

"Oh, it's okay. You're on Hanson, right? I can figure it out."

"Okay," I said, disappointed at losing an excuse to call her. "See you at seven."

"See ya," she said, I watched the graceful way her dark hair moved as she walked away. For a few minutes I was frozen in place, then I followed her, wanting to keep her with me even if it was only for a little while. I knew where she was parked. When I caught up, she was tossing her jacket into the backseat.

"Hey," I called, "have you started your paper yet?"

She looked at me, lost.

"For Gleason, I mean." She grunted, as if not wanting to be reminded. "What's your topic?"

"Labor unions." The words sounded like tasteless porridge.

"Be grateful," I said. "Mine's antitrust law." She opened the driver side door and slid in. "Hey, listen," I said. "I'm heading for the library. Why don't you come with me?"

"I think I'll pass. I'm in no rush to get into it. But thanks."

I knew by the sound of her voice that she wanted me to stop there, but I couldn't. "Well, how about a soda then?" I said, leaning into the passenger side. She retreated without even having to move and her face went lifeless. "Hmmm. A movie Saturday?"

"Mike . . ."

"Maybe we could get away for the weekend? The Bahamas don't cost much." That made her smile finally and I didn't fight its effect on me. "We could go steady, first if you insist. Or would you rather we were engaged?" She was laughing now and I said, "You're not easy to please, are you?"

"Mike, listen. I like you a lot. I like talking to you and I like hearing your stories, but I'm no good at that stuff."

I didn't know what to say, but I didn't want to leave it like this. "I like being with you. That's all."

"I like you too." She looked away, then back at me as if she were trying to explain something to a small child. "It wouldn't work with me, Mike."

I opened the door and got inside. She sighed, a little exasperated. "We could let me decide that," I said.

"Mike, give it up. Let's not spoil things."

"Are you back with Ron?" I'd heard she and Ron Bishoff had broken up almost three months ago. I knew it was a bold question, but I had nothing to lose at this point. I'd already made a complete fool of myself.

"I'm not back with anybody, Mike," she said, and started the car. "Let's leave this alone, okay?"

I said so long and let myself out, convinced that if I were someone else, someone normal, it wouldn't have had to turn out that way.

The first few kids arrived and he still wasn't home. My stomach was knotted, my head ached. I couldn't hear the things people said to me. My mother had put some pretzels out with cheeses and slices of apple, as if she couldn't decide if we were a fraternity or a bridge club. She stood in the dining room, hawking the street through slats in the blinds. I knew what she was thinking. She'd get to him first before he got inside the house.

After the rest of the kids got there, Melanie began reading a poem. I didn't hear a word of it. After everyone had talked to her about it, she looked at me and said, "You thought it was awful, didn't you?"

"What?" I said, lost.

"You hated it."

"No. No. It was great."

"People don't have to comment if they don't want to," Jack said. Tires screeched to a stop out front and my mind went numb. My mother hurried out to the driveway.

"Karen has something to read," Beth said.

I felt sick, dizzy. The car door slammed and I could hear my mother talking to him, warning him. That would set him off for sure. I knew it.

"The rain slashed against the loose shutters," Karen began her story. "The boys held their breath." My father's voice got loud outside and I saw a look pass over Beth's face. "They had only one candle left and no matches . . ." Karen's words trailed off. There was the heavy sound of a struggle against the front door, my father yelling, my mother's small voice, attempting reason, then the door opening. For a time, Karen kept reading and each of us sat frozen in place, afraid to look at one another, afraid to acknowledge what was happening. "Get off me, just get off my back." My father's shouts filled the house, made the air in the room brittle and unbreathable. Karen stopped reading. My mother coaxed him downstairs, still shouting.

"Listen, eh, I'm sorry," I said.

Nobody answered me or looked at me. Then something crashed downstairs and Melanie jumped up, with a frightened cry. Then more shouts rose from below.

"We better go, Mike," Beth said. I nodded. By the time they got their jackets on and got out the door, the place sounded like a Three Stooges movie.

I followed them out and sat down outside at the foot of the driveway, clutching my notebook, watching each of them walk away. They walked fast, wanting to leave me as far behind as possible. I didn't blame them a bit. Beth was the only one left. She stood in front of me, hesitated, then placed her notebook on the ground beside me and sat down on it. She pulled her knees up under her chin.

"Well, that's the end of that," I said.

"End of what?"

"The group. For me at least."

"Only if that's what you want." She waited, but I didn't answer. "It isn't what *I* want," she said. The kindness opened me, made me feel clean, a person apart from this chaos. I thanked her, but the words choked me.

"Want to talk?" she said.

I didn't answer. I stared straight ahead.

"You can't let it get to you, Mike," she said.

"Forget it. This is nothing new for me." I sounded angry at her, although I didn't mean to.

"For me either," she said. I sat frozen for a second, then

looked at her. She was staring down at her sneakers, as if the words had slipped out and it was too late to get them back.

"Things get like this at your house?" I couldn't keep from sounding amazed.

"For as long as I can remember."

I was confused. Beth was one of the perfect people. Smart. Pretty. Beautiful house. Friends. "You could have fooled me," I said.

"Yeah, I guess I could have, but where is that getting us?"

We watched the passing cars light the darkness, listened to bits of my parents' voices rise and crash in waves, an exchange with no purpose, no connection. I didn't believe Beth could know how this felt. Nobody could know how angry I was, how empty. It wasn't possible.

She touched my arm lightly, hardly making contact, but I couldn't say any more. Finally, she got up to go. She straightened the legs of her jeans and I handed her her notebook. "If you want to talk, come find me," she said.

I watched her walk away, like the others had, her notebook clasped tightly against her chest. For a moment I thought I had no choice but to let her go. I stood to see her better and watched for a long time. The notebook got heavier and heavier in my hand, a weight of secrets, years piled onto years, an aloneness so dense I saw now that I might never lift it off. My parents' voices faded, until they were lost in the night. The yellow tulips that lined the sidewalk glowed in the moonlight as if they were holding candles inside. Beth's head was bowed in a kind of sadness, or loss maybe, and I'd nearly reached her side before I realized I'd been running, before I knew that I'd already decided which story I would read to her.

As Skinny Does

Adele Griffin

Like many other young women who came of age in the eighties, my best friend, Holly, and I were nourished on that decade's crop of supermodels. Kate Moss, Naomi Campbell, Christy Turlington, and Linda Evangelista were our incontestable idols. We papered our bedroom walls with their airbrushed faces, we copied their hairstyles, and we promptly purchased whatever they were selling that minute; quick-dry nail polish, long-lash mascara, boot-cropped denim, or bikini-cut underwear.

It seemed that everything they had, we needed, and everything they seemed to be, we tried to be. Perfection was not unattainable, we hoped, not if we factored in the computer enhancing, retouching, and refinishing that went on in the back offices at *Vogue* and *Glamor*. Definitely, we could look like that, if we unearthed this perfect lipstick or sampled that cure-all hair conditioner. The difference between them and us must be simply a matter of *striving*.

And so probably it stood to reason that crash-dieting was one of the lesser-known and more dangerous activities that went on at our school. Girls would try any weight-loss plan, from lowfat grapefruits to nonfat cotton balls, in addition to the standards—smoking, taking laxatives or appetite suppressants, and of course plain old-fashioned starvation.

In this story, while the rivalry between Janine and Liz is souped-up and fictionalized, it underscores the hyperfocused and competitive attention to body image that I well remember from that time.

It was during our sophomore year that sweet sixteen parties swept through Sadtler Academy like a plague. They hit once or twice a month and were, at best, a chance for us to get out of our uniform kilts and into mixed company. Usually it went this way: The party-giver invited Sadtler's entire sophomore class, plus the entire class of Hill, our neighboring boys' school, to her backyard or rec room for a casual afternoon of standing around listening to music and eating grilled cheese sandwiches and birthday cake. The dress code was flexible, the gift was optional, and the highlight of the afternoon was when a couple of the Hill guys started wrestling or broke something, or both.

And so when Kim Willis, Sadtler's unofficial class princess who lived a house as big as the town library, decided to host her own version of the sweet sixteen, her mailed invitation was a triple shock.

> DRESS: BLACK TIE
> DINNER: 8:00 PM
> PLEASE BRING A DATE

"It's only three weeks away. We won't be able to find boyfriends in time," I despaired to my best friend, Janine. "I didn't meet anybody at the last sweet sixteen."

"There's always Freddie," she answered. Freddie was Janine's cousin, and she and he had been pinch-hitting as escorts for each other ever since Freddie's bar mitzvah a few years back. And Freddie, along with just about every other guy at Hill, was anxious to get to Kim Willis's party any way he could. Freddie would go with her, Janine explained, and he would bring his best friend, Jeff Donnelley, for me.

"But Jeff Donnelley's never said a single word to me," I wailed. "And we've been sitting in the same row in driver's ed every Saturday for the past six weeks."

Janine answered with a tired cough. She had been in and out of school with mono for the past month, and it was lucky her mom was giving her permission to go to Kim's sweet sixteen at all.

"Liz," she said, sighing patiently, "if you take Jeff, it's easier to us to ditch him with Freddie. Which leaves us free for you-know-who." You-know-who was Tony Willis, Kim's older brother, who Janine and I both spent most of seventh grade crank calling. We were too mature for cranking now, but more the idea of breathing Tony Willis's air made my heart somersault.

"Besides," Janine continued patiently. "We've got worse problems to think about. Like what to wear, and how to lose enough weight to fit into it."

"Like you need to lose any weight," I grumbled. "You're a stick!"

"You're a stick, too!" she said.

"No, *you're* a stick!"

"No, *you're* a stick." But I definitely was not a stick. I stood a full head over petite Janine, and recently my feet had stretched past a size ten.

Neither of us owned anything close to formal wear, and so we made plans to hit the Ridge Pike Mall that Saturday, allowing for a full afternoon to find just the right thing. For most of us, Kim's party marked the first occasion where we had been asked to wear a dress. Since my parents thought the idea of a formal sweet sixteen party was ridiculous, the expense was coming out of my own savings.

"Why don't you wear something of mine?" my mother asked. "It's crazy for you to waste your money."

Mothers can be so oblivious.

Meantime, the whole sophomore class had caught the fever. In and out of school, Kim's party took up pretty much all conversation, and was the subject of most of the note passing, too. As the party drew nearer, rumors abounded. Casey McGuire had been to the tanning salon five times. Kelly Renaldo was borrowing her aunt's silver fox fur. Cate Devigne was going all the way to Philadelphia to get her hair done. At dinner, I related these and other stories to my less-than-impressed parents and my four younger brothers.

"Liz, I don't want hear one more thing about this revolting, needlessly extravagant birthday party," said my insensitive father. "In fact, I think you should boycott it on principle."

So, at least during family hours, I tried to keep my mouth shut. Poor Janine had worse problems than a fed-up family; for one thing, her mono lingered and refused to go quietly. She was allowed to cut sports, and she took naps in the infirmary at lunchtime, and she never seemed to have enough energy for anything. She had lost a lot of weight, too, which left her looking wan and depleted.

"But you'll be okay for Kim's, right?" I asked, finally confronting Janine with the dreaded question in homeroom that Monday before thc party. The thought of Kim's party without Janine was too terrible to bear. I could hardly picture myself: Alone with silent Jeff Donnelley at the buffet table, alone with silent Jeff on the dance floor, alone with silent Jeff, period, and no Janine to whisper with about him.

"I don't know. I just wish I'd stop feeling so awful," she said. She did look pretty bad, I thought privately.

"But you're still going, right?"

"Mom says if I come home straight from school all week, and if I drink plenty of liquids, and I'm really careful about saving my strength—"

"Hey, there, girls!" We turned around to see Kim's best friend, unofficial sophomore class Barbie doll Kelly Renaldo standing in front of us. She was regarding Janine with an expression that I did not understand at first. It took a moment for me to realize that it was a look of frank admiration.

"Hi, Kelly," we chorused, but Kelly only had eyes for Janine.

"Whoa, Janine," she said, "I had to come over, cause I've got to say it! You look way amazing! What have you been doing to yourself?"

There was a silence, as both Janine and I contemplated

whether or not Kelly was putting us on or setting us up. Janine and I were not exactly the dork mascots of our class, but we were not automatically exempt from any practical joke that someone as cool as Kelly Renaldo might try to play.

"Well, uh, nothing," Janine said guardedly. "I haven't been doing, uh, anything much."

"It's just that you look so good! So *skinny*!" Kelly burst out. She turned to me enthusiastically. "Doesn't she? You must be totally jealous!"

I looked over at Janine. "Mm," I improvised weakly.

"Renaldo, are you telling Janine how be-*yond* thin she's looking?" Now Kim Willis herself had popped up on Kelly's side. To me, she said conspiratorially, "Me and Renaldo were talking about it on the phone last night. I mean, how did she do it?"

"Are you taking Slimfast? Protein bars? Just plain barfing, or what?" Kelly flipped up her kilt and squeezed the top of her little leg. "You've got to let me in on it. Look at me. I'm just *rolling* in fat!" She turned to Kim. "I tried it on again this morning, but I'll never fit into my dress for your party. What's your secret, Janine?"

"It's no secret. I just cut out some fats. I needed to, for my dress," Janine said, looking Kelly square-on. "But I'm almost down to the weight I want."

"Lucky you!"

"Yeah, go, Janine! See you Friday!"

"Why did you say that?" I demanded when they had gone. I poked Janine's bony shoulder. "What if Kelly hears that you have mono? Then she'll know the real reason why you're so skinny."

Janine shrugged. Her face had turned a pleased proud pink. "Oh, who cares?" she said. "It's kind of funny, isn't it? Like, here I've spent the past few weeks feeling worse than I ever did in my life, and now I'm getting compliments on it from people like Kelly Renaldo. That's just so funny."

"Sure, funny," I agreed. Although the emotion that

squeezed the tip of my heart was closer to jealousy than amusement.

For the rest of the day, I watched Janine from a refreshed perspective. Kelly and Kim were right—Janine looked great! How could I not have noticed her hollowed cheek and collarbone, the bloodless complexion, the way she had to double the waistband of her kilt so that it wouldn't fall down around her knees? She looked like a supermodel! She was going to be so scrawny and dazzling at Kim's party, and I would be fated to the role of the jolly, forgettable friend.

There was only one solution: the Starvation Plan. I had no choice but to match Janine, pound for shed pound.

Immediately, I went to my locker and tossed my brown-bag lunch, a peanut butter and fluff sandwich. (My kid brothers and I all split lunch-making duty, which meant I ate more than a fair share of fluffernutters, their favorite.) Later, at lunchtime, I watched and copied Janine, from the half-sips and sighs she breathed over her bowl of chicken noodle soup, to the final disinterested push of her tray.

"I'm exhausted," she said a few minutes later. "I think I'll go take a nap in the infirmary."

"Me, too," I said. A nap sounded good, and crackers and soup did not feel like enough to get me through the afternoon. Unfortunately, I was denied entrance to the infirmary on the grounds of good health. During track practice, though, I started to feel a little faint. I fell asleep on the bus coming home, missed my stop, and had to walk the half-mile home. My stomach was dying for a restorative snack, but a trip to my parents' full-length bedroom mirror revealed that I had not lost any noticeable weight, and a hop on the scale confirmed it.

That night at dinner, I ate a mere saucer of pasta, but in a house full of boys, all the food disappeared before anyone noticed that I had taken next to nothing for my portion. "You're quiet tonight," my father mentioned. "Did that silly dress-up party get canceled, I hope?"

Fathers can be so irritating.

By the next morning, my stomach rebelled. It churned and growled, demanding that I feed it. I drank some orange juice and swallowed a handful of Cheerios. This must be how the supermodels lived, anyway. All for the good of the cause.

I drifted through classes, trying not to think about pizza and hamburgers. At lunch, I sampled a mousetrap portion of cheese, and drank it down with a carton of skim milk.

"Are you on a diet?" asked Janine.

"I think I've just lost my appetite," I said.

"Well, I know how that feels," she said. "I used to think that when my mono was over, I'd gain all my weight back." She nibbled the edge of a salad crouton. "But it feels like I've permanently shrunk my stomach."

"Yeah, me, too," I said. "I guess I'm just not as interested in eating as I used to be."

On Wednesday morning, the scale at home claimed that I had lost a pound, but the locker room scale denied it. I skipped lunch, and while an afternoon pop quiz in chemistry left me with a terrible headache, I did sense a pleasant scooped-out-ness in my bones. I took an aspirin that did not sit well on an empty stomach. Finally, I fell asleep in the library and missed track practice.

By Thursday morning, I had lost a pound on both the school and home scale. Reinvigorated, I drank a diet soda for breakfast. My chemistry paper came back with a 66 percent. I was too light-headed to care.

"Did you know," asked Janine, watching as I ate some celery and saltine crackers for my lunchtime feast, "that this shirt I'm wearing is from seventh grade? I fit into it now. Isn't that funny?"

"Do you know," I returned, "I had to find my last year's track pants, since my new ones are so baggy?"

"You don't look any skinnier," she said, her eyes narrowed, surveying me up and down. "Did someone *say* you looked skinnier? Like Kelly Renaldo or anyone?"

I shrugged mysteriously.

That evening, I tried on my formal dress and, with a rush

of joy, noticed a slight gap between skin and fabric. The triumph overwhelmed all other petty concerns, such as my grades and health.

Friday morning, I overslept and missed the bus. My father had to drive me to school.

"Liz, you look a bit pale," he said. "If you want me to pick you up after lunch, call me at work, and I'll drive you home." This, from Dad, must have meant that I appeared close to death.

"If I have to come home this afternoon, can I still go to Kim Willis's party tonight?" I asked.

"Absolutely not," he snapped.

So I did not call. Instead, I wafted through classes, counting down the hours until lunch, when I could eat my two rice cakes seasoned with a packet of soy sauce.

"Two rice cakes?" asked Janine. "I don't think I could manage more than one."

"I'm saving the other for a snack," I said. "You don't look so good. Are you still going to Kim's?"

"Yeah, but my dress is so baggy. I wish I'd had it taken in."

"I know what you mean."

Janine and I had arranged that I would get ready for the party at her house, since mine always had a bellowing brother underfoot. At the time, it seemed like a fun idea. But when my mom dropped me off at Janine's, I discovered that she had already changed into her dress and was lying in her bed, reading fashion magazines.

"I'm a little tired," she explained. "All I've eaten today was an apple and some sugar-free gumdrops."

"All I've eaten is an apple and one rice cake, and I feel okay."

"Well, everything I ate, I threw up."

"Me, too," I lied. Janine eyeballed me suspiciously.

The photograph that Janine's stepdad snapped, just before we left for the party, shows us sitting stiffly side-by-side on the living room couch. I'm staring straight ahead, while Janine's gaze drifts down at the carpet, as if she might want to roll off the couch and nap there. We look about as ready for a party as we do for a week of detention.

When Freddie and Jeff pulled in, they were in such high spirits that they did not notice that Janine and I crackled with less energy than wet spaghetti. Freddie had a brand-new driver's license and was anxious to test out what his mother's station wagon could do, while Jeff had brought along a demo tape of his favorite hard rock band. They stayed up front, while Janine and I took the back. The music screamed from the speakers, and every time Freddie braked, my empty stomach flipped over. On my left, Janine slumped. Her eyes were closed and her brand-new drawstring evening bag dangled limply from her fingers.

We turned up the long, grand driveway that marked the Willis property.

"Oh, man," said Freddie. "I've been looking forward to this party *all day*!"

"Me, too!" said Jeff.

I did not even want to think about how long I had been looking forward to it. Next to me, Janine gave a damp little sigh, and I knew she was thinking the same thing.

Music and laughter drifted from a distance, and the air smelled greenly of spring. When we walked around back, it was a wonderland, with linen and silver set tables arranged out around the pool, and all the trees twinkling with tiny white lights. A live band was playing, and a few couples already had started to dance in rustling pairs on the custom-built parquet dance floor.

I spied Tony Willis and a few of his friends standing by the bar in the corner, looking bored and hunky. Listlessly, I nudged Janine's elbow; listlessly, she nudged back.

"Liz, you want to dance?" asked Jeff, the first words he had ever spoken to me.

"Um, not now," I answered. A headache was coming to roost behind my eyes. "Maybe later."

"Let's go sit over there," Janine suggested, pointing to two chairs at the far end of the patio. "I'm too tired to talk to people. Do you mind?"

I didn't. My head hurt too much too talk, anyway, and I had no spare energy to use up on enjoyment. I tried to concentrate instead on the feel of my ribs against the fabric of my dress when I sucked in my breath.

Fred and Jeff soon drifted away from us in exchange for the company of some other girls, of the smiling and talking variety. It seemed as if everyone was having fun, dancing and chatting and strutting around in the finery of moonlight and formal wear.

"I feel awful," I confessed after a while.

"Me, too." Janine looked at me mournfully.

"I'm too sick to have fun."

"Well, I don't need to stay here another minute," said Janine. "I'll go if you go."

"We could call my mom," I suggested. "If you're sure."

"Liz," she said, leaning forward, "I'm really, really sure."

So we sneaked inside and upstairs, where we found a spare bedroom, and we placed the secret call. Within minutes, my mother had pulled her car discretely to the end of the Willis driveway.

"To be honest, I was half waiting for the phone to ring. I didn't think either of you would last," she said as we drove away from the lights and music. "Neither of you looked up for a dinner dance."

"I think I'm just a little . . . hungry," I confessed.

Janine nodded agreement.

Mom asked no questions, but I got her infamous whale-eye, which meant that she was on to me. She took us on the junk-food loop: McDonald's, the video rental store, and the 7-Eleven, where I bought a gallon of ice cream and Janine bought two bags of chips to go with our greasy cheeseburgers and king-sized fries. Back at my house, we exchanged our dresses for sweatpants and spent the rest of the evening watching movies and eating gooey, cheesy, sloppy, salty, fattening junk food.

By my second bowl of ice cream, my head had cleared considerably.

"I kind of have to make a confession," said Janine, after

we polished up the rest of the ice cream and had moved on to tuna fish sandwiches, packed with pickles and potato chips. "I think I got addicted to being skinny. It made me feel so good, until it made me sick."

"Well, I think I got jealous," I admitted. "Especially after Kim and Kelly told you how good you looked."

"We missed the party of the year," said Janine mournfully.

"And one of the most perfect opportunities, ever, to talk to Tony Willis," I added.

"I'm never going to look at another fashion magazine again," said Janine.

"Me, either," I vowed. "I'm not built for skinny."

I would have liked to report that Janine and I stayed true to our vows and promptly tore down the photographs of our supermodels, and never again did I tried to lose weight. But other diets came and went, and the models stayed up on the walls, an endless reminder that perfection was a simple matter of starving.

Not that future diets were that easy. In fact, I had to sort of sneak them by. Because from that night on, whenever my parents caught wind of my future dates or big nights out, it always seemed that the kitchen was particularly chock-full of grocery store spoils. Whether they had brought home a pint of ice cream, or a tub of fried chicken, or some other high-calorie delicacy, it always proved a little too delicious to pass up.

Parents can be so sneaky.

Kids in the Mall

Mel Glenn

"Hey, man, workin's like school—only worse. You don't get off for Christmas."

If the world of school holds promise for future employment, the world of work, for teens, exists in the here and now. Teens work in a variety of jobs for a variety of reasons, the principal reason being money—money to save, money to spend.

When I was a teenager—seems like the last century—I worked, too. From the boardwalk in Coney Island where I sold hot dogs and knishes, and spun cotton candy, to a Brooklyn hospital where I counted pills in the pharmacy, to a camp counselor where I hit an endless number of fly balls and line drives to eager nine-year-olds, I worked to have some money in my pocket and hope in my heart that Roberta Wallin would let me take her to the movies.

Seasons change; friends change; classes in school change, but the need for work never changes. It's there with bosses, coworkers and neon lights. And the hub for working, at least where I live is the Plaza, a two-story pancake of a building that houses over two hundred stores.

Teens work there, the percentage increasing especially during the holiday season. These are teens from my fictional Tower High School. These are some of their stories:

SHANNON DALE,
REPORTER, *CITY STAR TRIBUNE*
ON ASSIGNMENT

Can you believe my editor?
Can you believe what that man is doing to me?
He might as well send me to
Shopping Siberia,
Mall Mauritania,
Plaza Patagonia.
I'm going to be
Hanged by holly,
Tortured by tinsel,
Eviscerated by evergreen.
All for what?
The usual "Teens Run Amok in Mall"?
or "100 Neediest Cases"?
Let me stay on my police beat, that's all I ask.
Instead he wants to send me to some
Mildewed, moth-eaten, mismatched,
Sad-sack series of stores and interview
Some verbally challenged teenagers.
Where the hell is Tower Plaza anyway?

**CONNIE TEDESCHI,
INFORMATION DESK,
STUDENT, TOWER HIGH SCHOOL,
FIRST-FLOOR CONCOURSE**

"McDonald's? Down the concourse, turn left."
"The Gap? Over on the left, halfway down."
"Radio Shack? Down the concourse, turn right."
"First Look, Men's Clothing? Behind me, to the right."
"Sir, I've told you three times already, I don't know."
"Ma'am, I can't say which is the best restaurant here."
"Son, I don't know if Santa has your list. He's over
there, go ask him."
It's crazy around here this time of year.
People rushing, grabbing, pushing, shoving,
All over the place.
They're all in pursuit of the Holy Grail of the Perfect
Present,

And they expect me to point them in the right direction.
If you ask me they've all lost their sense of direction,
As if the sign to Bethlehem is the same as the sign to Sears.
I can't wait for my shift to end,
So I can go soak in a hot tub with the door locked,
And nobody asking me a damn thing.

ERIC LEVIN,
SANTA CLAUS,
STUDENT, TOWER HIGH SCHOOL,
FIRST-FLOOR CONCOURSE

My mother yells at me,
"You had a Bar Mitzvah, how come you're playing Santa Claus?
God will strike you dead.
Did you tell your father?"
I am determined to keep looking for
Some person or passion to make my life meaningful,
So what is wrong with that?
I have just found a job in the service sector,
Where I can sit down, where I can listen to people,
Where I've discovered there are a lot of people
A lot worse off than me.
My mother yells, "God will punish you for this sacrilege."
"God will reward me for this service," I say.
How about a picture of me with a kid on my knee?
I'm sure my mother will flip out when she sees it.
What newspaper did you say you were from?

ANGELIQUE MARTINEZ,
TOWER HIGH SCHOOL CHORUS,
STUDENT, TOWER HIGH SCHOOL,
FIRST-FLOOR CONCOURSE

Thank you, you're very kind to say that.
You really liked our singing?
We worked very hard in rehearsal.
My favorite Christmas song?
That's easy.
I love "The Little Drummer Boy,"
Because he had no gifts to bring,
Except his music, of course.
When I sing with the chorus,
I close my eyes and imagine
I'm in Bethlehem singing for the baby Jesus.
But when I open my eyes I'm back in the mall,
Wondering if anyone hears the words,
Above the ring of cash registers,
Above the cries of "Is this item on sale?"

SHANELLE HENRY,
STUDENT, TOWER HIGH SCHOOL,
OUTSIDE, "EYE OF THE BEHOLDER"

I don't know why I'm hangin' out here.
I don't got no money to buy *any* Christmas presents.
But it's better to look at the clothes in the store
windows,
Than to listen to my teachers at Tower go on and on.
I'm thinkin' maybe one day I'm gonna open up my
own store,
A cool clothes outlet for kids,
Some place where they wouldn't get ripped off.
I see what they're sellin' at the *Gap*,
And I think I can do better.
I'm on pins and needles,
Waitin' for my life to bust out of
The gray pattern I've been walkin' around in.
You watch, one day I won't be
Hangin' on by a thread.
I'll be right up there with
Oleg, Calvin, Yves, and Donna.

It's part of my great design for the future.
To change the fabric of my life.

Annie O'Donnell,
Student, Tower High School,
First-Floor Concourse

After an hour with my parents,
I'm ready for the Witness Protection Program.
They constantly pinprick me with questions:
"Where are you going?"
"What are you doing?"
"When are you coming back?"
It's enough to drive me crazy.
So I escape to the mall
Where I can lose myself
In the anonymous aisles
And at the countless counters.
It's fun to window-shop
And plan my wardrobe and my flight
For the day I tell my parents
I'm leaving their house and their questions
For the largest mall in the world.
I hear it's someplace in Minnesota.

Matthew Mancini,
Assistant Manager,
Student, Tower High School,
Photo Op Camera Exchange

I hate this job.
Do you want double prints or an extra roll of film?
Do you want to actually buy a camera
Or just keep wasting my time with dumb questions?
How many shots of snow angels and Christmas
  stockings can you take?
Are you sure ten rolls of film are enough?

Is it possible to feel the Christmas spirit without
snapshots from every angle?
Tell me, is it conceivable to enjoy the Christmas
season
Without proof-positive of dozens of negatives?
Picture this:
A Merry Christmas without long lines, charge cards,
And countless presents bought out of a
sense of obligation.
Put away the flashbulbs, dead batteries
and forced smiles.
Come on, shoppers, let's bring this season into
Proper focus.

Caitlin Darrow,
Student, Tower High School,
Bell, Book and Candle

As the candles burn in the shop,
I sometimes think I am two people,
Both reflected in the soft light of the flames,
One, the nice little girl who attends mass,
The other, who hardly believes God exists.
I can't wait to get out of high school,
With its locked prison persona and stifling conformity.
Once you free yourself of the gravitational pull of
school
You can explore the galaxy of your own choosing,
And discover your own private karma.
I work part-time here at the *Bell,*
More hours now that spirituality is in season.
I sell candles and tarot cards
To people who hardly believe in anything,
but say they do.
What kind of life am I leading?
What kind of truth am I looking for?
What can I possibly learn
From a school system that has exploded and died,

Like some celestial nova long ago?
I hope the star of Bethlehem will forever shine
bright and clear.
If it's really there, that is.

**DUNCAN CHILDS,
STUDENT, TOWER HIGH SCHOOL,
FIRST-FLOOR CONCOURSE**

I don't read the papers no more,
Too much violence and stuff.
I don't go to the movies no more,
Too much killing and stuff.
I don't hang out in my neighborhood no more,
Too much drugs and stuff.
I like it here in the mall.
There's nice stores, nice girls,
And all the junk food you can eat.
People are usually cool,
But sometimes you get a crazy dude
Who sticks his face into your business, man.
But I don't worry none 'bout that stuff.
If anybody messes with me,
I just kick his ass.

**CICI VAUGHN,
SALES ASSISTANT,
STUDENT, TOWER HIGH SCHOOL,
FIRST LOOK, MEN'S CLOTHING**

When the boss first hired me,
I thought he was nice,
Too nice.
When the salesman on the floor looked me over,
I felt I was the merchandise.
At first all the attention was flattering,
But then it got kind of old.
"You got a boyfriend, kid?"

"You could model, you know that?"
"You and me, lunch tomorrow?"
"You want some help in the storeroom?"
These from men who look older than my father.
Was there anything they could do for me?
More like what I could do for them.
I need to keep my job, but I don't know.
Working in a men's store is not like what I thought.
Maybe I'm just not suited for it.

MIKE SIKORSKY,
EX-STUDENT, TOWER HIGH SCHOOL,
FIRST-FLOOR CONCOURSE

The first time I ran away from home,
I was fourteen.
I got as far as Philadelphia.
The next time I ran away from home,
I was fifteen.
I got as far as Norfolk.
The next time I ran away from home,
I was sixteen.
I got as far as Miami.
I learned how to hitchhike, steal food,
And get beat up.
There were times I went without eating at all.
And it seemed the further I ran, the less I got.
Now I just hang out here at the mall,
Minding my own business, looking for pretty girls.
Sometimes I sweep out some of the stores.
I tell you, it's a lot safer here,
Chillin' in one spot,
Instead of spreading myself out
All across the country.

ROBERTO PALACIOS,
STUDENT, TOWER HIGH SCHOOL,
CAPTAIN COOK SEAFOOD RESTAURANT

Why do you wish to speak to me?
Are you from Immigration, no?
From the newspaper, *sí.*
My English is not too good.
I often do not go to school
Because I must send money home to my relatives.
My manager, he also from Guatemala.
He teach me the business.
It's all rush, rush, rush,
With so many people eating alone.
Not like in my home country
Where Mamá prepares the biggest meal you can imagine,
And all the relatives come over to eat—for days.
How can Americans eat fast food for Christmas?
Do they not like their relatives?
Feliz Navidad, may your family be well.

**JAYNEE ALLEN,
STUDENT, TOWER HIGH SCHOOL,
FIRST-FLOOR CONCOURSE**

My father, having grown up in a small town,
Hates the malls, especially at Christmastime.
"I'm gonna get out of the city, buy some land," he says,
"For when you finish school, you know."
"Sure, Dad," I say, looking at the bright store windows.
When I was five, he promised me a rabbit.
"What's a rabbit gonna chew, wallpaper?" I said.
When I was ten, he promised me a pony.
"Who's gonna clean up after him?" I said.
When I was fifteen, he promised me a tractor.
"You gonna plant seeds in the living room?" I said.
"Could be," he said. "You're my best sprout."
Now, a year later, we walk slowly through the mall,
His hip bothering him, so we sit down when we can.

"You wait and see, Jaynee, one day
We're gonna be in the fresh air, riding horses."
"Dad, we're lookin' for presents for Mom, remember?
You think you can mosey on down to one more
  store?"

TOMMY DELANEY,
STUDENT, TOWER HIGH SCHOOL,
SECOND-FLOOR CONCOURSE

Last spring,
My dad took me to the auto show.
I never saw so many beautiful cars in my whole life:
Lamborghinis, Porsches, Bentleys.
I asked my dad whether he could buy one.
He laughed and said, "I wish."
This winter,
My dad asked me what I wanted for Christmas.
I presented him with my A list:
Mercedes-Benz E320, BMW 5211, Acura 3.5RL.
"Pretty expensive," he said. "Anything in
  a lower price range?"
I gave him my B list:
Jeep Cherokee, Ford Explorer, Chevy Blazer.
"Still pretty expensive," he said. "I'll see
  what I can do."
"Aw, Dad, come on, you can swing it.
How much can a remote-control car cost anyway?"

JANICE GREEN,
COUNTER,
STUDENT, TOWER HIGH SCHOOL,
RONDELL'S SPORTS STORE

If all my dates were horses in a race,
They'd all fight for last place.
I definitely have the knack for picking losers,
The slowest, dumbest, meanest animals around.

Dates consist of helping them with *their* problems.
If I were to meet a young man with
Good breeding,
Intelligent eyes,
Excellent disposition,
(Hardly likely 'round here),
He would probably race far ahead of me.
And I can't stand to be
Just another also-ran.
Hey, who knows,
One day I may get lucky and
Pick a winner.
Don't bet on it, though.

Nicky Roselli,
Student, Tower High School,
Second-Floor Concourse

My mother made me break up with my boyfriend.
She said I was too chronologically challenged.
Tony is eighteen, I'm fourteen.
She said there was no way she would allow
An eighteen-year-old to ravage me.
I asked her what "ravage" meant.
"Look it up," she told me.
"Didn't you meet Daddy when you were fifteen?" I asked.
"That was different, I was in love," she said.
"But Tony is not like . . ." I started to protest.
"Here's some money," she interrupted.
"Go down to the mall
And do some Christmas shopping. Forget about him."
So here I am,
Down at the mall, talking to you.
I can't believe she gave me this much money.
This large present I bought?
It's for Tony, of course.

David Hollander,
Student, Tower High School,
Outside, House of Leather

My father's hands are cold with contempt
When I play the wrong notes for him on the piano.
My father's hands are warm with applause
When I play the right notes at the recital.
"Practice makes perfect," he says, cliché-ridden.
"Play the melody in your heart," he says, anatomically
acute.
"Music will take you everywhere," he says,
geographically vague.
How far will it take me from you, I sarcastically note.
At home, at breakfast, we nod to each other
over coffee and bagels.
Only when we sit together at the piano,
And play a duet are we in accord.
See the gloves I just bought for him for Christmas?
They are to keep his hands warm.
Take note, Father,
If you continue to score me with criticism,
I just might close the musical book on our relationship
And drift away like some old, half-remembered tune
Heard at our family piano years ago.

Nelly Wallace,
Salesperson,
Student, Tower High School,
Doggie in the Window

Arf!
"How much does he cost?"
"What kind of dog is he?"
"How much will he eat?"
"Can I pet him?"
"Will he bite?"

At Christmastime everyone wants a puppy.
Kids pull parents by the hand into the store,
Hoping to pull a puppy by the leash out of the store.
"Can I please have him?"
"He'll be a good watchdog."
"He can sleep in my room."
"I'll walk him, I promise."
"I'll never ask you for another present."
I love it when a kid finds a puppy
And the puppy finds a new home.
To me, that's Christmas—no bones about it.
I know I will never get tired of
Puppy Love.
Arf!

**EVE MATERA,
STUDENT, TOWER HIGH SCHOOL,
SECOND-FLOOR CONCOURSE**

Excuse me, ma'am, I didn't see you,
Not with all these presents I'm carrying.
Do I have a minute?
A student, yeah, I'm a student, over at Tower.
What do I want for Christmas?
You're kidding me, right?
Well, let's see:
A cold wind outside, a warm fire inside,
And most of all,
I want my boyfriend, Larry, to say
  how much he loves me.
But that's *so* not happening.
These presents *are* nicely wrapped, thank you,
  did it myself.
For him? Not a chance.
I'm taking all these all back to the stores.
We just broke up—after a huge fight.
Yeah, I know, a real bummer.

He ruined my Christmas this year.
I hope he hasn't ruined my life forever.

**Steve Catera,
Student, Tower High School,
First-Floor Concourse**

Excuse me, ma'am, I didn't see you,
Not with all these presents I'm carrying.
Do I have a minute?
A student, yeah, I'm a student, over at Tower.
What do I want for Christmas?
You're kidding me, right?
Well, let's see:
A cold wind outside, a warm fire inside,
And most of all,
I want my girlfriend, Carrie, to say
  how much she loves me.
I hope that *so* happens.
These presents *are* nicely wrapped, thank you,
  did it myself.
For her? You bet, all of them.
I'm taking them over to her house right now.
We made up—after a huge fight.
Yeah, I know, so cool.
She made my Christmas this year.
I hope she'll make my life forever.

**Stephanie Ingram,
Counter,
Student, Tower High School,
Bunderful Burgers**

My mother doesn't like Marcus.
She figures I could do a whole lot better.
"He's only going to give you hamburgers and
  heartburn," my mother says.
"The musical selection will be from *Grease*.

For the wedding vows you'll exchange onion rings,
While promising to love, honor and cook for each
 other.
You'll honeymoon at McDonald's 'neath golden
 arches,
And in time there will be a little bun in the oven.
Honey, listen to me, he's telling you nothing but fries."
"Cute, Ma," I say, "but stop grilling me,
 I love my Marcus."
I see him every day here on my shift.
Hey, girl, don't you be talkin' to my man.
You orderin' the whole menu or sweating my baby?
Put a fork in it, you're done,
Or I'm gonna have to wipe the table with you.
Marcus is mine, my favorite dish.
Oh, you're with the newspaper?
Sorry . . . Next.
You want fries with that, sir?

Marcus Williamson,
Grillman,
Student, Tower High School,
Bunderful Burgers

I wear a uniform that makes me look like
 a Red Cross Volunteer.
I wear a hat that makes me look like a dork.
I wear an apron that makes me look like a housewife.
This job is an insult to my ego and my wallet,
But you know the old problem:
You can't get work without experience,
And you can't get experience without work.
So, I'm stuck here, fryin' my brains out,
But my dreams haven't gone up in smoke.
I am saving money to buy my girl, Stephanie,
 a really great present,
And my boss is really a cool guy.
I don't have no beef with him.

He wouldn't mind me talkin' to you.
This gonna be in the papers, really?
My girl's gonna flip over that.

KEVIN WINTERS,
STUDENT, TOWER HIGH SCHOOL,
SECOND-FLOOR CONCOURSE

What am I getting my family for Christmas?
Which family?
The one I live with now,
Or the one I used to live with?
What am I getting for my father?
Which one?
The one I live with now.
Or the one I used to live with?
In the years before the divorce,
When angry words flew like heart-piercing arrows,
I armored myself by not taking sides.
In the custody battle, my mother won, but I lost.
So now my biological father comes to our house
Every other weekend or when he can make it.
He asks me a lot of general questions.
I give him a lot of general answers.
What do you get both fathers for Christmas,
When your loyalties and money have to be divided,
When you have to put presents under two trees?

DEANNA BEELER,
STUDENT, TOWER HIGH SCHOOL,
SECOND-FLOOR CONCOURSE

One more hymn of humiliation,
One more refrain of regret,
One more chorus of cries.
The music stopped when
I dropped my boyfriend a year ago,
Just about this time, right before the holidays.

I caught them at a club together,
Their matching smiles, their touching hands,
All showing I was out of step
With what was goin' on behind my back.
When I got him alone, he said,
"We were only dancin', hon."
"You used to dance with me like that," I cried.
Now I miss his hands around my waist,
Slow dancin' to the music of our lives.
Tinny Christmas carols over the mall's loudspeakers
Cannot replace the sweet record of what we had,
The song of love in my heart,
Static and all.

Sharon Ortega,
Register,
Student, Tower High School,
Foods International

My math teacher tries to help me by joking.
"Sharon, are you on the five-year high school plan?"
My science teacher tries to help me by nagging.
"What is it, Sharon, why are you always late?"
My history teacher tries to help me by pleading.
"Sharon, please, please, get to my class on time."
I'm too tired to tell them all I'm too tired.
Is it my fault I have to work
A forty-hour week to bring some extra money
  home?
Is it my fault I have to work here in the mall
Until my father's new business deal works out?
I try not to think about all these money matters
As I add up the prices for frozen corn and
  stalks of celery.
When will it register that all these vegetables,
All these cans of soup, all these chicken parts,
Are eating out a major portion of my life?
Will I have to stand at the head of this

Slow-moving, coupon-bearing line forever?
I should just take this job and bag it.

RICHARD ARLETTE,
STUDENT, TOWER HIGH SCHOOL,
SECOND-FLOOR CONCOURSE

For eleven years at home
I listened to my mother,
And did whatever she asked.
For eleven years in school
I did my homework,
And put my book reports in clear plastic binders.
But in my twelfth year I discovered
Girls, freedom and hangin' around down at the mall.
Around the holidays, especially,
I can pick up some mad girls,
Chill with 'em,
Have something to eat,
And listen to some cool music comin' out of the
stores.
Now, in my senior year at Tower
I don't do any homework at all,
An advanced case of seniorities, I call it.
My mother now yells at me all the time,
But I don't have the time to listen to her.
I'm too busy, runnin' around the mall,
Listenin' to the only voice that matters.
My own.

JAMES LEE WARREN,
WAITER,
STUDENT, TOWER HIGH SCHOOL,
THE COFFEE CUP

What can I do for you, Miss?
Just coffee?
Right.

Sure I can't get you anything else, a Danish, maybe?
Just coffee?
Right.
What kind?
We have coffee from all over the world.
Do you know old coffee beans are called "has-beans"?
What are you writing there?
Sorry, I didn't mean to butt in.
No, I am *not* hitting on you.
Seventeen, eighteen next month.
Well, you can't blame a guy for tryin'.
You know the Christmas spirit and all.
I like older women.
Sorry, I didn't mean it like that, no offense meant.
Just coffee?
Right.

Freddie Bowers,
Salesperson,
Ex-Student, Tower High School,
Sneak Attack

When I dropped out of Tower last year
I told my folks they could use the money
They had saved for my college
And buy me a ticket for the coast.
I told them I would live with my Uncle Ralph
And play beach volleyball and get a job.
"You'll be back in a month," they said.
To prove them wrong, I stayed out there for a year,
Bumming my way from one resort to another,
Picking up the odd job here and the odd girl there.
Now I am back home, working at a sneaker store here
in the mall,
Pretendin' I'm still free,
Pretendin' I'm still an athlete,
Pretendin' the world really needs
Another line of magical high-tops.

Maybe next year I'll get my equivalency diploma,
And take a few courses at the community college.
I'll try to pull myself up by my own
Sneaker laces.

LEON BUCHWALD,
SALESPERSON,
STUDENT, TOWER HIGH SCHOOL,
BARGAIN BOOKS, INC.

Which books are people are buying for Christmas?
Oh, witch books and other best-sellers.
But if you ask me, all the great books are
  just outside the store.
Come, I'll show you; I have a break now:

Great Expectations	Maternity Clothing
Grapes of Wrath	Fruits and Vegetables
The Good Earth	Natural Foods and Vitamins
Billy Budd	Floral Arrangements
Gulliver's Travels	Luggage Company
The Scarlet Letter	Stationery and Art Supplies
The Time Machine	Fine Watches and Jewelry
The Turn of the Screw	Home Hardware Supplies
Lord of the Flies	Pest Control
Invisible Man	Weight Reducing Center

See what I mean?
Classics all.
I gotta get back, Merry Christmas.

JULIA PATRICK,
STUDENT, TOWER HIGH SCHOOL,
FIRST-FLOOR CONCOURSE

The evening stretches out like a lazy cat,
As I wonder through the stores
  on the first-floor concourse.

Everybody here, me and the rest of the crew,
As I play my tunes on my Walkman,
As I take a long sip of my Diet Coke.
I have time, all the time in the world to think of him.
My beauty created a bridge linking me and him forever.
I was able to cross over to his side of the tracks.
My life has turned wonderful, for real.
You can find me here any old afternoon after school,
Shopping up a storm,
Seeing my friends,
Checking out the CDs.
Christmas, you want to know about Christmas?
It's the best holiday of the year.

Patrick Julia,
Student, Tower High School,
First-Floor Concourse

The dawn stretches out like a lazy cat,
As I pick up the garbage on the first-floor concourse.
Nobody here, but me and the rest of the crew,
As I play my tunes on my Walkman,
As I sneak a quick sip of my Bud.
I have time, too much time to think of her.
My drinking created a river separating me and her forever.
I was never able to cross over to the dry side.
My life has turned to garbage, for real.
You can find me here early in the morning before school,
Picking up trash,
Mopping the floor,
Washing the windows.
Christmas, you want to know about Christmas?
It's the worst holiday in the world.

ANGELA HOLIDAY,
STUDENT, TOWER HIGH SCHOOL,
FIRST-FLOOR CONCOURSE

As I walk through the mall,
Putting the finishing touches on my Christmas shop-
  ping,
I think of my grandfather and the gifts he gave me.
He gave me words, beautiful-sounding words like
Susquehanna and Monongahela,
Special Christmas-wrapped words like
Theodora and Adirondack.
"Here, Angie, go find them on my wall map," he
  would say,
As my parents fought in the apartment downstairs.
"Here, my angel, go find them in my dictionary," he
  would say,
As the ugly words from downstairs grew louder.
I found beautiful words like confluence and cormorant,
Also funny-sounding words like
  doodlebug and doohickey.
The words and places stayed with me
Long after my grandfather left us.
I try to find the places on his map,
The map which now hangs in my room.
I try to use the big words he taught me,
Always in context, of course.
Merry Christmas, Grandpa, I love you.
Merry Christmas from the mall.

SHANNON DALE,
REPORTER, *CITY STAR TRIBUNE*
ON ASSIGNMENT

As I walk through the mall,
Putting the finishing touches on my story,
I think of what I've seen, what I've learned.

No bold headlines screaming rape or murder,
No extra editions announcing flood or famine,
But teenagers going about their business,
Working, wondering, worrying and waiting,
Trying to figure out their places in the universe,
Trying to figure out if and when their lives
Will take off and blaze through the sky,
Like some shooting star.
Some working hard, others hardly working.
Some waiting for love, others loving waiting,
For the ride into the upper atmosphere of adulthood.
The mall appears as a blip on the teenage radar screen,
An exercise in suspended animation.
No screaming headlines here,
Just teens waiting at ground zero, each with a story,
Just teens going about their business waiting to launch.

Testing

Tamora Pierce

When I began college, I was in the middle of a five-year case of writer's block, so I made other career plans. I chose psychology, with an eye to working with kids, structuring most of my work-study jobs to that end. I took education and social work courses as well as psychology. Just before the start of my junior year, my writing returned to me. After that, I forgot my original goal. I wrote.

After I finished the manuscript of a long, single adult novel titled *The Song of the Lioness*, I drifted, until my dad and stepmother invited me to live with them in Idaho. A week following my arrival, I found a job in the only thing I was educated for: I became a housemother in a group home for teenaged girls. Many events in "Testing" actually happened to me, though not all in the first week.

My girls were lively, inventive and well-defended. By the time I met them, their trust had been abused so often that it was hard for them to open up. I began a dialogue with them not through photographs, as X-ray does, but through storytelling. My first "serial" for the girls involved retelling my *Song* to them (I wasn't allowed to let them read my novel, which dealt with adult subjects). A year later, when my agent suggested that I break *Song* up into four books for teenagers, I realized I already had.

I miss the girls still. They taught me so much, not just about writing for kids, but about the need for a sense of humor. I've been trying to pay them back ever since, not directly, since we all fell out of touch, but by trying to help other kids who could use some fantasy in their lives.

I never realized how much I needed things to be *steady*. The Smithton Home for Girls wasn't paradise, but it was solid. Things had been the same ever since I arrived. Every other week we had Renee, who was the best housemother for a crew of ornery girls that you could imagine. She was perky, funny, energetic, knew the current groups and dances, and didn't yell at us to turn the music down during free time. We liked our other housemother, Shoshana, too, but in the spring of my first year at the Home, Shoshana got married and moved to Oregon.

They hired Dumptruck first. She was forty-something, sloppy, had a voice that would break glass, and feet she always complained about. To go from Renee to her every other week was more than any of us could stand.

Then we found out Dumptruck hated lizards. Hated snakes. And the way she yelled when she found the newt in her bed . . . She killed the newt with her shoe and quit. Keisha cried about it for days. You wouldn't think a girl who got sent there for robbing convenience stores with her thirty-year-old boyfriend would care what happened to a slimy newt, but Keisha was nuts for animals.

Next came Sugar. She was younger, thin like a stick, with dry straight hair and pale eyes that grabbed a girl and hung on to her. She carried a Bible wherever she went. We called her Sugar, after her strongest curse, "Oh, sugar!"

She told us to walk and talk quietly. She prayed before meals, which majorly chapped Maria Hightower. Maria's boyfriend taught her Native American religion before he got her pregnant and dumped her at a bus station. When Sugar insisted on prayer even after Maria explained about the Great Spirit, Corn Woman, and Coyote, Maria told us Coyote ought to teach Sugar respect.

By then we were tired of going from Renee, who made us feel good, to Sugar, who told us that the Smithton Home was our road to redemption. It was her not-so-subtle way of telling us that we'd all done stupid things to end up there.

Sugar was a little harder to get rid of than Dumptruck, but we managed. We painted some candles black, and switched the King James Bible she kept in her purse for a book Elsie found, *The Satanic Bible*. We wrote "Satan" backwards on the covers of our notebooks. Maria told her the baby the state made her give up for adoption was really sacrificed to the Dark Powers. Sugar ran like a rabbit.

I was drawing in my room a few days after Sugar left when Ana came to get me. "You got to hear this," she said. She led me to the office downstairs. Maria, Keisha, and Alouette were already listening at the closed door.

"—don't dare tell them they have control over which housemother stays or goes." That was Dr. Marsden—Dr. M., we called him—who ran the Home. "If we ask them to go easy on new housemothers, they'll be in the power position, and they'll use it."

"Sooner or later we'll run out of housemothers, Ben." That was Rowena Washington. Ro was the in-house social worker. She took us to court, medical, and dental appointments, helped the housemothers to chaperon at things like fairs and movies, and helped Dr. M. fill in when there was no alternate housemother. "Every time we advertise we get fewer and fewer applicants."

"They'll stop the testing behavior," we heard Renee tell them. "School's about to start—pretty soon they'll be busy with that, and they won't have time to get rid of the new housemother."

A chair scraped, and we got out of there. Later, in the smoking corner of the house, we decided "testing behavior" sounded like a most cool term for what we were doing. We would have put any new housemother through the mill, just as the girls the year before me put Renee through it, but "testing behavior" made it sound like an important kind of game. We *had* to play.

Five days later we came home to find a strange girl

sitting in the dining room with Renee. "This is Doreen Swanson," Renee told us. "She's going to be our new housemother." The girl—she was just out of college, we found out—smiled shyly as Renee started to introduce us.

I was shaking Doreen's hand when my throat started to close up. The minute she let go I ran upstairs to my room, and shut the door. I couldn't breathe. Sweat poured down my face; my knees wobbled so I could hardly stand. I dropped on my bed and covered my eyes with my arm, trying to get a grip. It was a panic attack, the first one in months. When I arrived at the home, Dr. M.—who was a shrink as well as the director—put me on tranquilizers and had personal sessions with me for weeks to help me with them.

Now I did what we'd worked out. I held my breath, then let it out slowly, the way Ana had to when her asthma got rolling. After a while, my throat relaxed some. I'm in my room, I told myself as Dr. M. had suggested. I'm on my bed. My stuffed animals are in a pile in the corner. My picture of my mom is on my desk. My books are on the dresser.

By the time I had named all the things that were mine, that had always been mine, the shakes were fading and I could breathe almost normally. I could think, which was the next step. I was supposed to work out what had given me attacks before. I didn't even remember what my last ones here at the Home were about. Before that, I got them in Juvenile Hall, in court, in cop cars and bus stations. I had one when the last guy who picked me up showed me his knife. Then it had actually been useful: he'd thought I was dying and dumped me out of his car. Those all made sense. Who wouldn't have panic attacks in court?

But this one came from nowhere, as far as I could tell. Those that hit without warning had been when I lived with my dad. Not while Mom was alive, not even when it was just me and him—no, wait. The first one came when I was maybe six. We had moved into a trailer home, our fourth house since Mom died. When I got off the bus I couldn't remember which trailer was ours. I'd had to sit by the mailboxes, sweating and trying to breathe, till Dad came home from work.

I didn't have another until he divorced his second wife and brought a new girlfriend home a week later. She bent down and grinned at me, showing big teeth stained brown. That night I woke up trying to breathe after a dream where she ate me. She was gone a month later. This time only two days passed before Dad introduced me to his new girlfriend.

That was when the attacks came all the time, whenever we moved and whenever he moved in a new girlfriend or a new wife. Aunts and moms, he made me call them, each one seriously bent somehow. What kind of regular woman would decide she was in love with somebody enough to move in with them after a night at a bar? Some took drugs, some made me do all the housework, some knocked me around, some had relatives or even other boyfriends who shared their bad habits and added a few of their own. It wasn't until I ran away that first time that I got a night's sleep, in someone's treehouse, with no panic attacks.

But for eight months at the Smithton Home, nothing had changed. Renee was there one week, Shoshana the next. The same faces, the same house. The same teachers, the same rules. The attacks slacked off, then stopped. Dr. M. took me off tranquilizers. And now I'd had an attack, over the newest housemother. The newest new face.

Maybe she'll stay, I thought as I washed up. Please let her stay.

Doreen was sweet, really, tiny, pretty and bashful. She survived all the tricks we played on her during her first week, and only lost her temper a couple of times. We wanted her to stay, but that was when Lydia Carmody still lived at the Home. Lydia had what the workers called "rage reaction." She would motor along quietly for about five weeks, then in the sixth week, boom! She would blow up and try to kill anyone who got in her way. She had her second explosion all over Doreen, who left with a broken arm and a broken nose. Lydia went to the state hospital. We were relieved about that, but sad about Doreen, and I had two mild panic attacks.

Jalapeño didn't stay either. She had a temper, and she hated to be sassed. We got her to lose her grip twice in front of Dr. M., and she went to work someplace else. Mrs. Bertoldi didn't survive her week of probation. She said that raising teenaged girls when she was thirty and raising them when she was fifty were two completely different things. Now I was waking up a couple of times a week, unable to breathe.

Penny was cool, *I* thought, but Elsie saw her sneak her boyfriend in through a downstairs window. That made Maria, Janice and Alouette crazy, because if the housemother could have her boyfriend over, why couldn't we? They called Dr. M., and Penny was gone in a day.

The next one . . . The next one. We called her X-ray, for the way she seemed to look right through you with her pale eyes. She was medium in almost everything, medium height, medium skin, medium chubby measurements. She spoke just loudly enough to be heard by the people around her, no louder. The only thing that would make people look twice at her was her hair. Even its color was medium, somewhere between blond and brown, but it fell all the way to her waist. When she wasn't dressed up for the interviews or for meeting the board of directors, she wore pants and shirts in colors no one would ever remember. We thought she maybe came from a planet of invisible people.

During her observation week, when she followed Renee around to see how things were done, we kept an eye on her. She seemed okay. When we sang in the van—we sang a lot when Renee drove us—it turned out X-ray knew some interesting songs we'd never heard before. She didn't even mind writing five copies of the lyrics out by hand, since the house computer was for house business or homework help, period. She didn't freak when Alouette sneaked up behind her and screamed in her ear, like Jalapeño did. On the coordination scale she rated about a minus fifty: even with Renee to help, we couldn't teach her to dance.

Keisha and I voted to leave her alone, the night before she spent her first week on duty with us. I was so tired of the attacks, and I knew sooner or later somebody would notice I was showering sweat off in the middle of the night again. They'd tell Dr. M., who'd put me back on tranquilizers. I *hated* those things. At school our first tests were due. Torturing the housemother took a lot of work we could use to study instead—and I wanted things to calm down. I wanted boring, excitementless days back.

"No way," said Maria. "She can't walk in here like them others and expect us to love her because she's, you know, taken an *interest*." Maria was the hardest of us and maybe the smartest. Her mom was a drunk, so she had looked after her brothers. That stopped when Children's Services put the kids in foster homes. The boys' family was okay, but Maria got a string of creeps, the same as Keisha and Elsie. I guess without her brothers to take care of, Maria ran a little wild, met her boyfriend, stole some cars and got pregnant. "We can't fall for that I-love-you-cuz-I-just-*do* crap," she added.

"Why don't you just go and put a two-cent price tag on us?" demanded Ana, checking her hair for split ends. "Tell 'em we're *easy*?" Ana thought she was such a hard case. All she ever did was sell pot at school until her folks got her busted.

"She gets tested the same as Renee got tested," Elsie said.

Testing X-ray won the vote. Keisha and I went to do homework while the others decided on a plan. The staff would be sure to warn X-ray of everything that was done to the other housemothers, particularly since we were all on restrictions for it. That meant no walking home from school: staff picked us up. That meant no TV during the week, and no mall trips till after Christmas. Of course, restrictions meant we had more time to work on the newest housemother. You'd think they would have worked that out.

Finally it was the first day of X-ray's first duty shift, and the rest of the staff had gone home. "Let the game begin," Janice whispered in my ear as we walked into the house after a cigarette break. I rolled my eyes, but there was no way I wouldn't do my bit, panic attacks or no. I had to live with these guys.

There were snacks and juice on the dining room table, so we all grabbed chairs and sat. Alouette dropped into the chair across the table from X-ray. "Where are you from?" She challenged X-ray in the way she said it; she wanted X-ray not to answer the question and to say Lou was rude. "You're not from around here."

"I moved here two months ago," said X-ray, peeling an orange.

"Where from?" asked Lou.

"College," said X-ray, getting orange skin oil on her face.

"And where was college?" That was Maria. She spoke in that bright, slow, hyperinterested tone that grownups who don't know better use on little kids.

I was sitting beside X-ray. Maybe I was the only one who saw the corner of her mouth quiver, as if she hid a smile. In the same understanding tone as Maria's, X-ray replied, "Philadelphia."

"Where were you from before that?" Elsie had a heap of Oreos in front of her. She was opening them, eating all the filling, and putting the cookies aside. She'd only eat the cookies when she'd sucked up all the filling.

"It depends," said X-ray. Keisha and Janice rolled their eyes. I saw X-ray glance at them, and there went that quiver at the corner of her mouth. "Right before college I lived in Singapore."

We all looked at each other. Who ever heard of someone living in Singapore? Who ever heard of a medium person like X-ray living anywhere cool?

"How'd you get there?" Janice asked. That wasn't part of the testing; she really wanted to know.

"My parents were in the State Department," replied X-Ray. "We moved around a lot."

"So where were you born?" asked Keisha.

X-ray frowned, as if she had to think hard to remember. "Guam, but we went to Peru right after that. We lived there till I was four, and then again when I was in high school."

"Peru!" Janice leaned closer. "What was that like?"

Now X-ray did smile. "It was all right, except for the volcano."

Everybody began to yell, wanting to know about the volcano and Peru. I thought maybe she was lying when she talked about walking all day with an umbrella to keep the ash off and a scarf tied over her mouth and nose, but she showed us a picture in her wallet. It was definitely her; definitely she had the umbrella and the scarf. From the waist down she was covered in ashes. By the time she got done telling us about how nice it was before the volcano erupted, it was time to start supper.

Now Keisha and I weren't the only ones who didn't want to test X-ray. Janice wanted to know about the places she had lived; she didn't want X-ray leaving until she'd heard it all. Janice was always writing stories in notebooks and reading about far-off countries with goofy names, telling us she'd go to them when she got out of the Home and became a rich writer. She thought she could get ideas from X-ray. Maria was determined to test, though, and when Maria was set on a thing, Ana, Lou and Elsie would back her up.

"No warning her," Ana told us while we finished

clean-up in the kitchen. At the Home, the girls cooked and cleaned while the housemothers supervised. "We never warned nobody else."

Maria excused herself from homework at the dining room table later and went into the kitchen. When she came back, she had an open-faced sandwich made of peanut butter and marshmallow fluff. I watched as she squeezed behind X-ray's chair, and stumbled. She brought the fluff-and-butter side straight down on that long, long hair, then dragged it all the way from X-ray's neck to the ends.

She immediately began to apologize, saying she was sorry over and over. Maria was the best actress in the Home, though we were all pretty good.

We held our breaths, waiting to see what X-ray would do. First she pulled her hair around in front of her and inspected it, a strange look in her eyes. "Oh, ick," she said finally. I could see she was breathing hard, and the corners of her mouth were tucked really tight, but she didn't blow up. Did Dr. M. and Rowena warn her that blowing up got you a failing grade on the test?

She went to the big mirror in the entry hall, using it to look at her hair in back. "I know I need styling gel, but isn't this kind of extreme?" she finally asked.

We stared at her.

"Aren't you mad?" asked Janice, wide-eyed.

"I'm not *happy*." X-ray replied, twisting to get a better look at the back of her head. "But I've had worse."

"Oh, yeah?" demanded Maria coldly. We all nodded. Who could believe that? "Like what?"

X-ray backed closer to the mirror, to see if she could improve her view. "Well, the girls in this tribe in Africa told me I wouldn't be cool till I did my hair like they did. They rubbed this orange clay all over my head and braided my hair. I couldn't even wash it out before we left the village, because it would have hurt their feelings."

We stared at each other, horrified. "For real?" Elsie wanted to know.

"I have pictures," said X-ray.

After a moment of respectful silence, Keisha asked, "So how can you ever get this junk out? You'll have to wash and wash and wash, and it'll be all gummy."

X-ray gave herself one last look in the mirror, sighed, and walked back into the dining room. "I just let it grow in college—I hate fussing with my hair. It begins to occur to me—" She looked at us, and something in her eyes made me wonder if she wasn't pretty sure Maria's stumble wasn't an accident. "—maybe my hair is a liability in a job like this. I'll end up using time I should spend on the job keeping it out of my face." She sighed again. "I'll tuck it up and tie a scarf over it for now, and get it cut tomorrow."

We all traded looks. The plan was that she'd run upstairs and jump right in the shower. We could stay up late and she'd never know, while she tried to get that gunk out of her hair. Now we were stuck and she hadn't even yelled at us.

"I cut hair good," Lou commented suddenly. "I used to cut my sisters' hair at home." Maybe she even had. Lou never talked about her real family.

X-ray bit her lip, and touched the back of her neck lightly. A hank of white and gold streaked hair stuck to her fingers. She tugged them free. "You sure?"

"Absolutely positive," Lou told her.

We scattered, some of us to find newspapers, Janice to get the tall stool, and others to fetch a towel and comb and to giggle in the bathroom. X-ray brought the good scissors from the office.

"Of course, it was a really long time ago when I cut hair last," said Lou as she chopped a big chunk right out of the middle of the mess. I saw X-ray's shoulders droop. Still, she didn't stop the party. Instead she told us about the photo safari that ended in that African village while Lou cut and Maria and I took turns wiping goo off the scissors. When Lou finished, we were all quiet. Poor old X-ray looked as if somebody had cut her hair with hedge clippers.

What she did when she saw herself in the mirror was important; we all knew that. It was like the moment when Maria smeared that mess over her hair: If she did a Jalapeño, we had her. If she started to cry, we had her. Particularly if she walked straight out the door, we had her. If she did the sweet silly thing and said it was a great cut, we'd know she was just another lying social worker pretending to be a friend. By the time we got to the Smithton Home, we had all had it up to here with people like that.

X-ray inspected the cut in Elsie's hand mirror, then went back out to the entry hall mirror. We followed her. Lou kept her hands over her mouth, trying not to crack up; Ana and Elsie were snorting. X-ray took her time viewing the damage. Again I saw the corners of her mouth tuck, first down and then, weirdly, up; her breath came faster for a while, then slowed. At last she said to Lou, "It could be worse—but not by much."

Lou ran upstairs, laughing so hard she couldn't breathe. X-ray shook her mangled head. "Let's clean up that mess and finish the homework," she told us. "And then it's getting on toward bedtime."

"Why aren't you mad?" demanded Maria. I think she was angry that X-ray kept all her feelings hidden. "I'd be mad."

"I'm upset," X-ray said, looking straight at us. "I'm human, and I didn't want to look like a dazed porcupine this week, thanks all the same. Still, the damage is done, it can be fixed. If I didn't learn anything else growing up, it's that you do better if you just deal and move on. When you keep meeting people from different cultures, you can get yourself in real trouble by losing your temper. Homework."

We got back to studying, and she went upstairs. When she came back down, she had wrapped a scarf around her head and made it into a kind of turban. We knew then she wasn't going to wash her hair until we were asleep.

Lou came down with her; when we looked at Lou to see if X-ray had yelled at her, Lou shook her head. "She said I might want to get lessons before I cut any more hair," whispered Lou when X-ray went into the kitchen for some water.

The next morning when Rowena came to drive us to school, I was the only one downstairs, setting the dining room table. I heard Rowena gasp when X-ray let her in. "My God, girl, what happened to your head?" Sometime the night before X-ray had shampooed what hair she had left, and gotten rid of the turban.

I couldn't hear X-ray's answer, but I heard Ro: "Dr. M. is gonna be pissed."

"No," X-ray said flatly, loud enough that I could hear. "I asked Lou to cut my hair—I don't want her getting in trouble for something I asked her to do. Besides, once I get it trimmed, it'll be easier to take care of."

"But aren't you mad?" I heard Ro ask, just like one of us.

X-ray laughed. "When you get back, I'll tell you something worse that happened to my hair once."

I told the rest what she had said on the way to school. Lou seemed thoughtful, as if maybe she was sorry she had done it now. If X-ray hadn't stood up for her, Lou would be on restrictions forever, we knew that.

But Maria was still the hard case. "She's just trying to suck up and make us her little buddies," she told us as Ro was paying for gas. "You wait. It's all a fake."

When we got home from school that afternoon, we found X-ray with her hair trimmed and shaped short, like a boy's. She actually looked okay. And she had stopped off at home, because a scrapbook sat on the dining room table. It was open to a picture of her at our age. Orange clay caked her head, turning a pair of braids she wore into orange turds. We laughed till we cried.

Then Janice wanted to look at the rest of the book.

Keisha and Elsie did, too, partly because they were interested—what was X-ray doing in *Morocco*?—partly because that was the next plan. I wanted to hear the stories, too, but I was in our latest test, never mind being up for two hours in the middle of the night with an attack. While the other girls kept X-ray busy, Maria, Lou and I sneaked out the back door.

Our yard was circled by a hedge six feet high. Nobody but girls or staff was allowed in there. Our boyfriends were right outside the back gate. We'd set it up at school. Lou and her boyfriend ducked low until they were past the kitchen and dining room windows, then went to the far side of the yard, where they couldn't be seen from the house. Maria and I stayed close to the gate, talking with the guys. I was too nervous to kiss Pete in front of other people, and Maria and Chuck weren't that far along yet. They were actually talking about books when X-ray walked through the gate. She must have left the house through the front door and come around the yard so quietly that we didn't hear her.

I never thought someone who was so medium could go so cold. Chuck and Pete actually seemed to shrink, even though they were taller than she was. "We—" Pete began to say.

X-ray pointed at the gate. "Out," she said flatly.

Chuck and Pete left. X-ray walked over to Lou and her boyfriend. They were so busy she had to tap his shoulder. When he looked around and saw her, he actually backed away from Lou. X-ray pointed to the gate, and he left.

Back came X-ray with Lou. We all went inside. When we got as far as the dining room, the other girls looked at us with horror. They told us later she'd gone to answer the phone in the office. They never saw her leave the building.

"I'd like to think the rest of you didn't know about this, but I'm not so sure," X-ray told us. "In any event, up to your rooms till supper, all of you. And you know

I have to report this to Dr. M." The way she said it, not even Janice tried to talk her out of it. We all knew the rules; there were no exceptions. And it had just occurred to us that medium-quiet X-ray could be strict.

On our way up the stairs Maria whispered in my ear, "She's quick, you gotta give her that."

We complained to each other. We swore we were running away. Elsie, who had a knack for being over the top, said the Home was just as bad as prison, though we knew it was no such thing. Maria had been in prison for a week; Keisha had been in jail for a month before they placed her in the Home. From what they said, we *never* wanted to go to a real prison.

We came down for supper, cleanup and homework. By then Dr. M. had arrived to give the lecture and hand down the punishment. After that, we went to our rooms.

Friday night was when the staff took us out for pizza, to the mall or a movie. With everybody on restrictions, Friday should have been a major pain, but it wasn't. X-ray showed us how to make stir-fry for supper. Then we had ice cream and she told us stories from the photos in her scrapbook.

"Why take so many pictures?" Maria asked as she paged through. "You have, like, all kinds just from Calcutta, and you were only there a week."

"I'm a photographer," X-ray said. "I like taking pictures. It gave me something to do when I didn't have friends to hang out with."

"So if you're a photographer, how come you're working here?" Ana wanted to know.

"Because everybody has to start somewhere, and I have to eat till I get rich and famous," X-ray told her. "I have to build my portfolio, to show what I can do. Besides, I took social work in college."

Maria ran a finger over a picture of a beggar who sat beside a soda machine. "Would you show us how to take nice pictures like these?"

"Yeah!" cried Elsie. "That'd be cool!"

We begged X-ray to teach us. She looked us over with a wary eye. Maybe she was remembering we switched the sugar for salt at breakfast, or that her *Evita* CD, that she had played for us the day before, had gone missing. "Tell you what," she said finally. "You'll have to find your own cameras, even if they're the throwaway kind. We'll start with that, and I'll develop your photos on my time off. Beyond that, we'll see."

Now we looked at the pictures in her scrapbook differently, asking her how she'd taken them. Friday night ripped by. We hardly remembered to be mad because we were on restriction.

We had to wait for the next test till Sunday afternoon, when we took our nature walk. Keisha really fought that—she was afraid X-ray would kill an animal. We finally talked her around, and on the walk she found a nice garter snake. We left it in X-ray's bed. Then we had to wait till bedtime. X-ray stayed downstairs for hours, it felt like, writing in the log. Then she climbed upstairs. We all went to our doors to listen.

Nothing.

Nothing.

Nothing.

Her light went out, and still nothing. Some of us waited till midnight, thinking we'd hear the scream any minute. We didn't hear a thing.

Keisha could be so dumb. She and Maria were on the schedule to fix breakfast. As soon as they got to the kitchen, where X-ray was starting the coffee, Keisha said, "You killed it!"

"Nope," X-ray replied.

"I don't believe you," Keisha said. She started to cry. "You killed it."

Maria said X-ray sighed and went upstairs. When the rest of us came down to breakfast, there was a shoebox with air holes punched in it on the kitchen counter. The snake was curled up inside, under some paper towels, with a jar lid full of water next to it. "I'm taking it back where you got it," X-ray said when we sat down to eat. "And shame on you for yanking animals from their homes for a joke."

"That's it," Keisha told us when we piled into the van for school. "No more animal tests. X-ray's right."

"Get us all in trouble, why don't you," muttered Janice as Rowena got in.

X-ray didn't report us or the snake to Dr. M.

"Everybody listen," Maria said when we met for a planning session at lunchtime. "No more of the test stuff till Wednesday. We hit her with everything on her last day."

"Why?" Janice wanted to know. "I like her."

"Me too," said Keisha.

I raised my hand. If X-ray stayed, maybe the attacks would stop. Things would be calm again.

Maria put her hands on her hips and glared at us. "We liked Penny, but she turned up wrong. And Mrs. Bertoldi just dumped us, 'cause we were extra work. We save it all for her last day, all right?"

So we were angels for three whole days, except for Maria and Ana getting in a fight over Maria's plum nail polish, that Ana said was hers. And Lou sneaked a long-distance call to her dad, who she still thought was going to take her back. Ro caught me smoking behind the work shed—more restrictions. Janice thought someone stole her cheapoid camera and ran around accusing everybody, but when we looked, it turned up in the mess under her bed.

Wednesday afternoon, when we got back from school, we hit the ground running. Even Renee got some tired by Wednesday. In their first couple of weeks new housemothers were always wrung out by the end of their shift, which is why we had saved up. At snack time, supper time and homework time, when we were supposed to be together in one room, a couple of us always made sure to be gone, so X-ray couldn't sit for five minutes without having to get up and hunt for missing girls. Our school friends called off and on all night, so X-ray kept having to run to the office to get the phone: they always hung up when she answered. Lou put a KICK ME sign on X-ray's back—just like Lou, so immature.

Just as homework time was ending, the phone in the office rang again. X-ray actually *growled*. We waited for her to walk into the office and close the door. Then Ana and Keisha, who were the strongest, grabbed the knob and hung on. Doors at the Home opened in—with those two on the outside, there was no way X-ray could escape. She rattled the knob, tugged on it, banged on the door and yelled, "Girls, this isn't a good idea." Ana and Lou hung on, giggling.

The office went quiet, and everyone but Ana and Keisha ran upstairs to do what they had planned. I was disgusted by the whole thing and went into the dining room to finish my homework. I didn't hear—nobody heard—X-ray pull the chair over to the window and open it. We found out later that she climbed out, quiet like a ghost, slipped under the dining room window, slid out the back gate, and walked around. I saw her when she very quietly opened the front door with the Home keys and let herself in. My jaw dropped. She held her finger up to her lips and walked, not tiptoe but still without a sound, down the hall. She waited until she was right behind Ana and Lou before she said, "Did you girls need something?," as if they'd never locked her in. They screamed, and jumped, and ran upstairs. X-ray went back into the office.

We had a snack before we went to bed, and a last look at the scrapbook. I couldn't help but think that if she quit, we'd never know about the islands that were just tree-covered rocks, eaten away by waves at the base, rising out of a perfectly blue sea. She wouldn't explain who the men in blue head veils were, or the women who wore masks that were made of coins. We'd never find out how to get to the buildings that were carved into a pink stone cliff. I'm pretty sure Janice was thinking the same thing, because she lingered over the scrapbook, turning pages with a gloomy look on her face. X-ray had to gently take the book from her and tell her it was time to go to bed.

We lay awake with the lights out once more, waiting for X-ray. When she came upstairs, we all went to our doors to listen. "Yick," was her only comment when she tried the doorknob at her room and found oil on it. It wasn't even a *loud* "Yick." She went inside.

We went to listen at her door, for what good it did us. She had to have found we'd soaped half of her toilet seat and honeyed the other half, just as she must have discovered we'd restuffed her pillow with old Easter grass and short-sheeted her bed. The problem was, if she did anything when she found all those surprises, it wasn't noisy. We heard a thing or two that might have been sighs—that was all. We gave up and went to bed once she turned out her light, after we did one last thing. We got macramé cord from the crafts room, a thick, braided rope of it. First we tied it around X-ray's doorknob, making sure it was tied tight. Then we pulled it across the hall, wrapping it first around Keisha's doorknob, then Maria's. We figured X-ray would go nuts when she found she couldn't get out.

I was up with an attack an hour before my alarm rang, so I showered and dressed. I figured it wasn't *so* bad: at least I could see what happened when X-ray tried to go downstairs. I tiptoed into Ana's room: if I watched through the door, holding it barely open, I'd get a view of X-ray's room. Ana didn't even stir when I came in—she slept like the dead.

I heard the muffled sound of the housemothers' alarm clock. Ten minutes later, I was half asleep when I heard a knob rattle. X-ray's door opened a bare inch, no more. The cord shook twice, as if X-ray had really yanked on the door. Then it eased.

She *couldn't* give up so easily.

The cord tightened again as her door opened as far as it would go. Then I saw a silvery gleam. A knife began to saw at the cord. Within seconds it fell to the floor, cut through. X-ray came out, looking tired. Calmly she folded up her penknife and stuck it in her pocket. Then she gathered the cord, undoing it from Keisha's and Maria's doors without a sound. She coiled it, yawned, stuck it in her pocket and went downstairs.

When we went to breakfast, the coil of cord was in the middle of the dining room table, like a centerpiece.

She said good-bye when Ro came to take us to school, waving as we pulled out of the parking lot. Ana settled back in her seat. "She won't come back," she announced. "She's worn out."

"So am I," Janice muttered.

"Yeah," added Keisha.

A week later, on the drive home from school, I got an attack. I tried to stifle it, doubling over my books. Keisha, sitting beside me, poked my arm. "You're having one of those things, aincha?"

"Shut up," I wheezed.

"You better tell Dr. M.," advised Maria from the seat in front of us. "You been doin' it a lot lately."

I gave her the finger. Maria didn't take it personally, lucky for me.

Ro pulled up in front of the Home and we got out. Everybody else ran in ahead of me. They wanted to make sure that they had won and X-ray was gone. I walked in slowly, trying to calm down, thinking that if this was winning, I sure didn't want to lose.

They all stood by the dining room table, silent. A new scrapbook lay there. We heard banging noises and peeked into the kitchen. There was X-ray, cleaning out the garbage disposal we had jammed at breakfast.

We all pulled back into the dining room, looking at each other, wondering what everyone else would say. Finally Maria sighed. "Aw, hell," she told us. "Let's keep her."

Not that we made it *easy* for X-ray to stay on, of course.

Thirteen Diddles

Jon Scieszka

I write things now the same way I wrote them when I was in high school. I get the assignment, forget about it since the deadline is so far away, panic when I suddenly realize the piece is due, drop everything else and despair that I'll never come up with a good enough idea on time, start six seven eight nine different things that look incredibly stupid the next day, then latch on to one piece of one idea that somehow takes root and starts to grow into something possible. A good percentage of these somethings usually die in the harsh light of rereading the next day, but if anything survives I add to it and tend it and tweak it and hope it springs to full life before I make some fatal slip of the pen and kill it.

And that's exactly how I wrote "Thirteen Diddles." It started as one little piece of one of many false starts and lame efforts. But somewhere in that wreck of prose, there was this little variation of the nursery rhyme "Hey Diddle Diddle" done as a string of insults. It was almost funny. And it reminded me of a book called *Exercises in Style*, by Raymond Queneau. The book is ninety-nine different variations on one small incident. It always cracked me up, and I always wanted to write something like it. This was my chance to write a mess of variations on one nursery rhyme. The variations could be kind of like schoolwork. There are thirteen contributors to this book, so I could do thirteen variations. It would be perfect.

Or at least it would be finished and I could turn my assignment in on time.

So what you have before you are the thirteen variations that made the final cut. I'd love to stick around and tell you more about the variations that didn't work, the nursery rhymes that didn't work, and the other strange works of Raymond Queneau and his friends in a group called the Oulipo, but I just remembered another assignment

I promised my editor I would definitely have finished by last week.

Ahhhhhhhhhhhhhhhhhhhhh!

1

Hey diddle diddle!
The cat and the fiddle,
The cow jumped over the moon;
The little dog laughed
To see such sport,
And the dish ran away with the spoon.

2

Ehay, iddleday, iddleday!
The atcay and the iddlefay,
The owcay umpjayed over the oonmay;
The ittlelay ogday aughlayed
Otay eesay uchsay ortspay,
And the ishday anray away ithway the oonspay.

3

BEEP

Hey Diddle. This is Kat. Fiddle is over here at my house and we were thinking of going to see that band tonight? Cow Over the Moon? Dog says they're pretty funny. Give us a call as soon as you get in. Otherwise I guess we'll just run over there with Dish and Spoon.

BEEP

4

Nouns
Cat, fiddle, cow, moon, dog, sport, dish, spoon

Verbs
jumped, laughed, see, ran away

Adjectives
little

Prepositions
over, with

Interjections
Hey diddle diddle

5

Date: Wednesday, September 1, 1999 9:37:07 p.m.
From: Hey@home.com
Subj: Good Luck
To: Ddiddle@aol.com

you have got to check this out. afriend of mine got it from a friend of his who works for microsoft or something and he swears itworks and youll get tons of free stuff because the government or somebody is doing research on websites an browsers or something.

Go to http://www.cat&fiddle.com
Click on either:

Cow jumping over moon
or
Dog laughing

Forward this e-mail to 10 friends and good luck will come your way. One person who received this message and didn't forward it came home and found all of his dishes and spoons gone.

6

Hey, (loiter, dawdle), (loiter, dawdle)!

The (mouser, swingster) and the (violin, Stradivarius),

The (bossy, heifer, Holstein) jumped over the (heavenly body, orb of night, piece of green cheese);

The (dinky, piddling, inconsequential) (pooch, cur, tail-wagger) (snickered, cackled, guffawed)
To see such (play, festivity, skylarking),

And the (plate, container, receptacle) (eloped, decamped, skedaddled) with the (dip, scoop, ladle).

7

My sister met this guy once who knew a guy whose friend had the weirdest thing happen to him. He's walking down the street late one night when he passes this alley and hears someone playing beautiful music. It sounds amazing, so he looks in the alley, and even more amazing—it's a cat playing a fiddle. The guy makes friends with the cat and they end up hatching a plan to get rich. The guy borrows everything he can to rent this club downtown. He puts up posters, calls everybody he knows, and packs the place at one hundred dollars a person to see the Fiddling Cat. The crowd is wild. The guy is richer than he ever thought possible. Then the curtain goes up. Nothing. The cat licks his paw and goes to sleep. The crowd goes nuts and just about kills the guy to get their money back. The cat, of course, disappears.

The guy finally makes it back to his apartment, pretty well beat up and freaked out until he flicks on his light. Then he's freaked even more, because there is his dog sitting on his couch watching Monday Night Football and laughing.

"Now I'm really losing it," says the guy. "First the Fiddling Cat fakes me out. Now my dog is laughing at TV football."

Then the dog turns around with the remote and says, "I wasn't laughing at football. I was laughing 'cause I just saw your last dish run away with your spoon."

I don't know exactly what happened to the guy, but something like he went totally mental and had to be locked up. And it's a true story, I swear.

8

A fiddling cat from Rangoon,
Once shot a cow over the moon.
Dog laughed, “How’d he do it?”
Said Dish, “Nothing to it.”
“Cold paws on the udder,” added Spoon.

9

LEO

Stop fiddling around with that unsupportive relationship. Trust in your own mysterious catlike ways. This powerful new you will have admirers swooning and enemies cowering as you jump over negative influences of the full moon early on the 7th. In the workplace, Mercury in retrograde around the 16th will dog you. Laugh at your fears. Try a new sport. Start a new hobby. Show the world you can dish it out, and love and happiness will be yours on a silver spoon.

10

Hey, diesel, diesel!
The catalpa and the fief,
The cowl jumped over the moor;
The little dogfish laughed
To see such sportwear,
And the dishrag ran away with the sporan.

11

In "Hey Diddle Diddle" the author attempts to show the themes that life can be amusing or that sometimes you have to run away from it all.

The cat represents curiosity. He plays on the fiddle like life can be played. The cow is a symbol of motherhood. The moon is a symbol of feminine nature. So when the dog sees all of this, he laughs because this can be what the nature of life is.

The dish and the spoon are usually next to each other on the dinner table and would seem to go together. Unlike the dog, who is *man's* "best friend," the dish and the spoon can't take the play of the feminine symbols in life and so they run away.

In conclusion, "Hey Diddle Diddle" powerfully shows the themes of what can happen in life symbolically sometimes.

12

Hey, to waste time, to waste time!

The small soft-furred four-legged domesticated animal and the stringed instrument played with a bow,

The fully grown female of any domestic bovine animal used as a source of milk and beef rose off the ground by sudden muscular effort in the legs over the natural satellite of the earth, orbiting it monthly, illuminated by the sun and reflecting some of its light to the earth;

The small in size, amount, degree, etc., four-legged flesh-eating mammal related to the wolf and fox made the sounds and movements usual in expressing lively amusement.
To perceive with the eyes such amusement, fun,

And the shallow-bottomed container for food went with quick steps, never having both or all feet on the ground at once away with the utensil with a bowl and handle for lifting food to the mouth, stirring, etc.

13

Hey. Diddle diddle.
Cat fiddles cow over moon.
"Run," says dish to spoon.

POP QUIZ

Name 13 possible variations on the nursery rhyme "Hey Diddle Diddle."

1. Original
2. Pig Latin
3. Phone Message
4. Grammar Lesson
5. E-mail
6. Thesaurus
7. Urban Legend
8. Limerick
9. Horoscope
10. Math Assignment n + 7
    (Replace each noun with the 7th word following it in the dictionary)
11. Book Report
12. Definitions
13. Haiku

Tell Me Who You Hang Out With and I'll Tell You *What* You Are

Eleanora E. Tate

I was inspired to write "Tell Me Who You Hang Out With and I'll Tell You *What* You Are" from my own strange interest in snakes. The title is a twist on the saying "Tell me who you hang out with and I'll tell you who you are," which I heard some years ago while making an author's visit in the Saginaw, Michigan, area. I decided to wrap a story around my interpretation of the meaning. It's about shape-shifting. Snakes historically, have gotten a bad rap from folks who fear them, but I—and my main character, Ravine (nicknamed "Red" for her red baby dreads)—find them fascinating. Of course, I get scared, too, when I see them in our yard here in coastal eastern North Carolina. But they're all God's creatures and have the right to share the Earth's living space. As long as they stay off my porch and out of my house!

One of Red's strengths is that she loves animals and wants to become a snake doctor. But sometimes a character's strength when overdone can become a weakness.

When a girl named Anna mysteriously shows up at school and immediately develops a crush on Ravine's best friend Jojo, Ravine goes overboard. Ravine, who has many theories on how things in life came to be, believes that the girl's "snaky acting" behavior means that she actually IS a snake, or at least has been one in a "past" life. Red tries in vain to warn Jojo about this creature, but he resists her warnings repeatedly until she's almost ready to give up.

Happy Reading!

I knew something was snaky about that girl from the way that she flicked out her tongue.

My best friend Jojo Tootle and I had been walking through the hallway toward Advanced Algebra class, minding our own business, when wham! This *girl* bumped smack right into Jojo's chest. Jojo's eyes got as big as headlights. He stared down into her oval, greenish-yellow eyes. Now, hard as it might be to believe this—with her so close—he hadn't seen that *forked tongue*! Couldn't have! Because by then she'd already marked him, so now he was froze!

"Yo yo, Jojo. Class. Algebra. Hello?" I had to pinch his bony arm through his T-shirt twice to make him move. He gazed around at me with those zombie-sized eyes. Finally I gave him a shove. Still fixating on her standing there, he stumbled on past toward algebra class, his head swiveling around almost backwards toward her like that girl's in that *Exorcist* movie.

It was not good for Jojo to be marked by something like her.

Hold up now. Jojo and I do not have a boy-girl thing going on. I was not trying to get Jojo away from Miss Snaky Face because I was jealous. Because I was *not* jealous. So what if she was tall and skinny, pale brown-skinned, wore that ebony-and-emerald-striped long-sleeved jumpsuit as tight as skin on a wiener, and had thick black and blonde-streaked braids (which I just knew could *not* be real) snaking down beneath her shoulders?

Whereas me. I'm what my momma calls "healthy" which means plump, with red baby dreads. I wouldn't be caught in anything tight with it ninety-nine degrees in this school, know what I'm saying?

Of all the people in the world, Jojo should have recognized that he had just been marked by a snake—order Squamata, suborder Serpentes. I'm talking scaly, long and wiggly, crawl-on-the-belly reptile kind of snake. After all, Jojo and I are snake doctors. I mean, I am. I mean, I plan to be a herpetologist—a biologist who specializes in studying reptiles and amphibians. Then I was going to be a reptile vet and specialize in treating zoo snakes and frogs. Jojo was just going to be a regular vet and treat dogs and cats.

We didn't have any anacondas or black mambas or boa constrictors to work on around here, of course, but we had enough redbellies, milk snakes, king snakes, black racers, garter snakes, swamp snakes, cottonmouths and rattlers in our yards and around our pond to keep us busy for years. Snapping turtles, pond sliders and yellow-bellied painted turtles were back there, too. Saltwater loggerhead turtles lived at the Aquarium nearby in Atlantic Beach. Plus, I had a reptile lab in my backyard.

Suddenly Jojo shivered all over like he was having a fit. Then he squared around to me with his face frowned up. But at least his eyes were normal-sized again behind his gold glasses. "Red, what's up with you, snatching me across the hall like that?" he said.

"Because you were trippin'. You had turned into concrete on the spot." I dropped my backpack and placed both hands on his thin (he's into weight training, okay, but the results haven't kicked in yet) shoulders. "When that girl bumped into you she marked you, my brother."

"You're the one's trippin'. That sister was fly." He shook me off and stretched out his neck like a turtle, still looking for *her* in the crowded hallway. "Shoot, she can mark me anytime she wants."

His words stung my ears. I shut up and followed him into Miz Withers' Algebra class. Dude was *still* trippin'.

Let me explain a theory I have, that I developed three years ago when I was eleven, that will explain this situation. I know that folks go to heaven or hell eventually, forever. But the ones about to go downstairs get a second chance. See, the Lord gives them instructions, and they're sent back to earth to try to do better—but in a different form. Maybe a beetle or an elephant. Or a snake. If they pass the test, they come back in a higher form, get born again, then die, over and over as they work their way up the food chain to heaven again. Incredible, huh?

If you looked hard at somebody you could figure out what form they might have had on earth before. Like, some folks who act sneaky, have pointed noses and maybe are even hairy might have been foxes or wolves or maybe even dingo dogs. Or rats. If they walk slinky with their heads hung down and laugh funny, they might have been hyenas. If a person walked r-e-a-l-l-y s-l-o-w, he or she might have been a turtle (order Testudines), or even a snail or a sloth.

When I looked at that *girl*, I saw a female snake.

I developed my theory after I saw a Don Knotts movie on TV where he played a fish. And later on when I saw him as Andy Griffith's deputy on *Mayberry, RFD* he *still* looked like a fish. So I thought about that and wondered, hmmmmmmmm, what if? I presented a paper entitled "Herpetological Manifestations in the After Life" for English class using my "what if?" argument and got an "A" for imagination. "B" for mechanics. As soon as Jojo and I get our Web page up, I'm going to publish my paper on-line. I like to watch everybody closely and ask questions because I'm collecting more data for a major paper to submit to the Association of Reptile and Amphibian Veterinarians Journal and the Audubon Society when I get older. It's all good.

I also got a theory about how Momma Earth "marks" or puts her flavor on every living thing growing on her. This theory is also based on fact.

Fact one: Me. My Mom had craved strawberries so much the month before I was born that she ate a gazillion of them. So guess what? My head's kinda shaped like a strawberry, I have a long thin chin (like Arsenio Hall and Jay Leno), a wide forehead, and a reddish-brown complexion, kind of like the color of a ripe strawberry. Plus, my dreads are red, like I said. Which is why everybody calls me Red. And I got a fiery personality. My real name is Ravine Avery. Ravine is romantic. Red is practical.

Fact two: Jojo has a curly black two-inch-long goatee on his chin. He was born with it just like that, growing on his baby chin. That goatee was more proof that Momma Earth can mark you *before* you're born, as well as after. Jojo's mother had a dream about a white goat with a long black beard. In that dream the goat chased her so long and scared her so bad that she went into labor and had Jojo. Who had a goatee. And that's a fact.

Jojo thought my theories were nuts. But not even Jojo could dispute his momma's dream.

In Algebra, I decided to watch him for any more signs showing that this girl had "marked" him. I liked snakes, of course—I might have been one in another life—but I wasn't comfortable about *this* one, and still so strong in a girl's body, know what I mean?

In the front seat by the windows Jojo sat winding his goatee around his right forefinger. That seemed normal enough. I stared at him intently. I had this special look that could make him know I wanted his attention. In a couple of minutes, he glanced over at me. Then he passed me a note by way of Jesse, to my cousin Taneshia, then to Shimmie, who dropped it under Zack's desk, who kicked it over to me. It said, "I got a baseball meeting, don't wait for me, help me cut our grass." That seemed normal enough, too.

I tried to relax and concentrate on what Miz Withers was saying, but this was Friday of Memorial Day weekend, so algebra was a drag! Everybody was headed to the coast, to us here in Morehead City, North Carolina, to swim, fish, and party all weekend. So were we! Tonight Jojo's folks and mine were having a big cookout in our backyards, and tomorrow our dads were taking us to the Aquarium.

The hands on the clock crawled. I yawned, drummed my fingers on my desk, and got a mean look from Miz Withers. I got into being a snake doctor because of Miz Withers' husband, who had been my sixth-grade teacher. I had never seen someone get so stoked over the difference between a lizard and a salamander than him. Mr. Withers knew so much about reptiles and amphibians that I expected to find his picture in a calendar or in some book about great African American biologists one day. He told me about some students in Minnesota who had found deformed frogs, and their discovery had set off a chain of international controversies about the environment and animals and pollution. Well, that got me going, too.

Algebra class snailed along and Jojo didn't do anything weird. I wondered if maybe I had made a mistake about that girl's tongue being forked. Maybe she just had a fancy stud in it instead. Maybe the vibes I got from her were leftovers from Social Studies class. That hurricane watch and warnings quiz I took could have made me supersensitive. I scratched at a dry spot on my elbow where I had bumped into Miss Snaky Face, and yawned again.

As soon as the bell rang, Shimmie and Taneshia and I pushed past everybody to our lockers; mine had pictures of king cobras and the schedule of my Squamata Club meetings glued to the front. When I turned around, whoa! I was scrunched up against that yellow, triangular-shaped face of Miss Snaky Face herself! "Where's he, where's he, where's he?" she spat through barely moving lips. I jumped back up against the lockers, my arm snapped across my face to keep from staring into the slitted pupils of her hypnotic eyes.

When she stuck out her purple-fingernailed hand to touch my arm, I swore I saw green scales under the cuff of her long-sleeved blouse. "I said, 'What's happening?'

"You're Red, right? I'm Anna. Anna Glide."

I peeked at her from under my arm and nodded slowly. Now she was smiling, showing perfectly straight small white teeth and round pupils. I couldn't see her tongue.

"Don't you remember me? I saw you earlier today, and I'm just saying hi. I'm in ninth, too, with you all. That boy you were with—what's his name? I want to apologize for running into him."

I lowered my arm a little. Her snake life vibe was still so strong I could almost see her slithering through the grass. "Oh, unh, hey, Anna. When'd you move here? How could you transfer so late in the year? Where you from? Do you have a stud in your tongue? Lemme see? Aren't you hot in that shirt?"

Shimmie and Taneshia had been listening and watching. Shimmie broke in. "Dang, Red! You sure are nosy! Hey, Anna, Jojo Tootle is his name."

"I *am* about to burn up, but I got this rash on my arms," Anna said. "Well, maybe I'll run into you all this weekend somewhere. Later." Sweeping her braids back over her shoulder with her hand, she turned away. Then she turned back and stuck out her plain, bumpy, ordinary average-length, red tongue.

Taneshia nudged Shimmie with her shoulder. "Shimmie, did you hear my girl Red grill her? Yeah, 'cause Miss New Thing's peeping on Jojo! Look, look, look, look, Shimmie! Red's blushing! Her earlobes are redder than her hair! And check out the cheeks!"

"Oh puh-lease." I flipped my backpack over my shoulder to hide my hot face from them. "There you go, Tam-tam, trying to start stuff. Don't even try it. You know I only ask questions in the name of research. See ya to-night." I hurried past them and everybody in the hall, and rushed out into the clean wet marshy air. I shook my dreads and wiped my forehead on my arm.

Traffic was already heavy on Bridges Street Extension where I rode my bike toward home. I could barely wait until eight o'clock tonight when folks would start coming over. Yet the question of why Anna bumped into Jojo and now wanted the 411 on him stuck in my brain. I soared around the corner onto our street. Did I really actually ask to see a stranger's tongue? Had I been studying snakes too much? Put Miss Snaky Face out of your mind, I told myself.

In a few minutes I was pushing the lawn mower around the pecan tree trunks next door at Jojo's house. Jojo's mom was bent over in her weedy flower bed by the carport. Slouched down in the seat of his dad's riding lawn mower, Jojo bounced over the little molehill tunnels. He drove with his right hand, his goatee twisted around his left forefinger. Well, that seemed normal enough, too.

Suddenly Miz Tootle let out a scream. When I looked around, I saw her leap out of the begonias with her hands clawing the air and land feet-first up on the carport ledge. "Snake, snake, snake, snake, snake!"

Man, that was a cool jump! I'd seen Miz Tootle move fast before, but not like that! Unlike her son and me, Miz Tootle despised snakes. "Where's that little ole snake this time?" I hollered over the noise of our mowers.

She pointed. I revved up the lawn mower and rolled it in that direction. Then I slowed down. On the lawn by the flower bed a snake had risen at least a foot up into the air, its head turned toward Miz Tootle. The rest of its thick blond, brown, black and green diamond-patterned body trailed in the grass for another two or three feet.

This was a big baby. No wonder Miz Tootle was shook up. I pushed the lawn mower at the snake to make it move.

But you know what? Instead of slithering away, it

slowly turned its shiny triangular head with its yellowish-green eyes toward me, flicking out its tongue, hissing. My heart thumped. Who could ever forget those eyes? I stared into them. It was that *girl* Anna.

"Red, Red, Red, kill it, kill it!" Miz Tootle's yell jarred me out of my trance. When I charged again at the snake with the mower, it dropped down into the grass and wiggled toward the front porch. "The door, the door, close it!" Miz Tootle was screaming and pointing at the screen door hanging ajar. "Get it, get it, get it!" With a quick turn of the mower, I cut off the snake's route to the porch. It wiggled across the lawn right in front of Jojo and on into the pyracantha bushes.

I shoved the mower under the pyracantha's prickly branches and bumped it around the base, then opened the throttle wider, increasing the engine's roar by a million decibels. The snake shot out from the other side of the bushes, undulating through the grass faster than even a black racer. But I flew right after it, with the lawn mower chewing up grass just inches from that brown, black and green tail. It disappeared into the rambling rose hedges growing along the edge of the ditch. I shoved the mower after it toward the ditch's edge, revving the motor a couple times, then turned it off.

Behind me Miz Tootle still stood on the carport ledge. When I waved at her, she slowly squatted and sat down, fanning herself with her hands, shaking her head.

"Jojo, Jojo, you in trouble, son," I shouted, dragging the mower behind me. "That snake girl is in your yard now, stalking you!"

"What?" Jojo had that same dopey look in his eyes like he'd had in the hallway.

"Wake up! That was her—that snake was Anna, that girl!"

I turned to his mother, who was tiptoeing fast as she could along the sidewalk to the front porch. "Miz Tootle, you're not gonna believe this, but—"

"No, and I don't wanna hear it, either." She reached

the porch and stepped from one foot to the other, peering around. "Was that one of you'all's pets got loose again? Jojo, if you're the cause of this, I'm not laughing 'cause it's not funny. You and Red better get rid of all those snakes and things before they turn on you! And Mr. Jojo, once I saw you with one all up around your face and neck, hugging and kissing on it. You're gonna contract some kinda snake disease!"

When I tried to tell her about that girl, she cut me off, saying, "No, no, no, I don't want to hear any more talk about snakes." Inside the house now, she talked through the screen door. "Jojo, Red, you stop cutting around here with that thing on the loose. Go in the back and cut. That was a water moccasin, and they're poisonous."

"Naw, it's not, Momma." Jojo came out of his trance. "It's just a garter snake."

"But have you ever seen a snake like that around here before? Didn't that look like that girl Anna?" I said.

"Red, the only thing I noticed is that if you'd got out the way I could have caught it, and then we'd know what it was. You're worse than Momma, chasing snakes with the mower like you gone wacko!"

My mouth fell open, then closed. I put my hands on my hips. "Excuse me? Your momma was scared and I was trying to help. What did *you* do? Sat up there with your eyes popped out!"

"Couldn't it have been a mutant? Maybe we found something new? But no, you're trying to traumatize it. You're the one's marked. Somebody marked your brain: 'crazy.' " Cranking up the lawn mower, Jojo headed for the backyard.

Well, what flew up his shorts? "You don't need to get so mean, you ole hard head thing, snapping at me, you ole snapping turtle, you ole Chelydra serpentina!"

But after I marched behind him to the back lawn and cooled down a little, I thought things over. He was right about capturing it. All I'd thought about was saving his momma, not about making a great discovery. Some herpetologist I was going to make. And sure, I've seen people who looked like they used to be animals. That was part of the "fact" aspect of my theory. I figured that I had past lives, too, but never anything as low down on the food chain as a snake. Still, if I was, I bet I'd been a local one, like an Eastern milk snake. It has my own red and brown colors and though it doesn't do milk it does eat other snakes.

But I'd never seen a real live animal that looked like or had once been a person. Which had always made for a major gap in my theory—until now, with Anna. But how could I prove this to Jojo? Or was I tripping, like he said?

As I mowed around the last pecan tree in the back, I was sure that I felt yellowish-green eyes burning into my back. I scratched my elbow again. That dry spot had spread a little. Maybe I had caught eczema. Or Anna's rash. I reminded myself to ask Mom what to put on it.

I finished just in time to check on my lab. Actually it was an old falling-down brick storage building with a couple of tables and some shelves. We didn't keep animals in the lab longer than about a week unless they'd been injured. The really sick or badly injured ones we took over to the wildlife shelter around the block from us. After we measured and marked them with a waterproof magic marker to track them later on, we let them go. A green, little grass frog (*Limnaoedus ocularis*) lived in Mom's green sprinkler can on the back step, a brown toad lived under the porch, and a green-and-black-striped garter snake liked to crawl around on the pump house roof. I counted them as "specimens in the wild."

When I came in, Jojo was dropping slices of bread and pears into an old claw-footed bathtub where Bob the baby snapping turtle and Larry the pond slider hung suspended in the water. Their cracked shells were healing nicely. Jojo looked up at me, then went back to feeding them.

Reaching into a closed glass aquarium, I lifted out

Adolph, the black snake. Its shiny black body curled around my arm. I had found it under a fallen tree limb with a cut on its tail. It was healed now and time for it to go back into the wild.

"You feel better now?" Jojo asked. "You stopped trippin'?"

"I was just trying—"

"*Stop trippin'!* I don't want you pulling and poking on me in public like you own me ever again. 'Cause you don't."

"If you had seen how stupid you looked, *you'd* have poked you, too!" was what I wanted to say, but I didn't. Instead, I just said, "Excuse *me*!" and "It's your turn to check in here tonight," and left the lab. I walked out to the pond and sat down on a tree branch where I'd found Adolph. Jojo had been acting strange for the last few days, so this girl couldn't have marked him back then. The last few days he had other things to do rather than be around me. He'd been snappy. Maybe he didn't want to be best friends with me anymore. What was wrong? Jojo and I had been best friends since playpen days.

Adolph flicked out its tongue against my cheek, then slid up around my neck. "What did you say, Adolph? What?" I held the snake close to my ear. "Maybe it's his hormones? Maybe he's having a testosterone attack? And you want to go home? Okay, okay."

Just before I set the little snake on the ground, I looked around. Nobody was watching. I lightly kissed it on its head. "Good luck. See you around," I whispered as it disappeared into the cattails.

As I headed back for my house, I scratched at my leg, where the itching seem to have spread. Maybe the best thing was to just leave Jojo alone for a while, at least until tonight, I decided. Maybe it was his hormones. Or he was probably in one of his moods. Maybe he'd also been marked by a mule. He could sure be stubborn like one sometimes.

* * *

Great-Aunt Grankie and Taneshia were among the first to arrive. She and Taneshia pranced up the sidewalk doing the Ashanti welcome dance Grankie had learned back in the day when she had lived in Ghana. Grankie swept me around in her arms. We three danced to the backyard where Mr. Tootle, Jojo and my dad were barbecuing chicken legs, beef ribs, hamburgers, hot dogs and pork chops. Mom, Miz Tootle and I had brought out big bowls of salad, platters of corn on the cob, thick chunks of garlic bread, and plates of chocolate cake squares. As soon as Daddy called out, "Come and get it!" Taneshia and I grabbed up plates. Jojo went off to eat by himself under a pecan tree.

"What's wrong with him?" Taneshia asked. I just shrugged.

Miz Tootle settled herself down by Mom and told everybody about me chasing that snake. "I meant to thank you, Red. Lordie, I liked to died when I saw it. But Betty," she said to Mom, "how your daughter and Jojo can stand to be around those things is beyond me."

"Well, you know that old saying, 'tell me who you hang out with and I'll tell you who you are,' " said Miz Garner, our neighbor from across the street. Miz Garner told me one time that I was weird because I liked snakes and lizards. She was always throwing out those old sayings, which I thought was weird of *her*.

"So what does that one mean?" I asked around a mouthful of potato salad.

"It means," said Mom, with a frown at Miz Garner, "that if you keep listening to Miz Garner you might end up just like her. So maybe it's 'tell me who you hang out with and I'll tell you *what* you are.' " Everybody went, "Oooo," and "Don't go there, Betty," but Miz Garner missed Mom's sarcasm and just nodded. I sent a grateful look over to Mom. Mom and Miz Garner didn't get along, either, partly because Miz Garner let her six dogs run wild, and they liked to come poop in our yard. We kids called her the dog woman. She was Great-Aunt Grankie's friend, anyway.

I noticed that Jojo had finally joined us on the porch.

"Anyway, the kids coming along today are new millennium kids," Daddy added. "They don't pay any attention to those old sayings and tales. They got computers and all that technology to explain everything scientifically."

"Unless they know when somebody's been marked by a snake," said Taneshia. She giggled and pointed at Jojo, who groaned. I slapped Taneshia on the shoulder to shut her up, but she didn't. "See, this really cute girl at school was looking at Jojo hard and Red got mad and said the girl was a snake and had marked Jojo and was chasing him. Tell the truth, Red, didn't you say that?"

"NO MORE SNAKE TALK AROUND HERE!" Miz Tootle shouted. The folks sitting in chairs in the grass laughed, but a couple of them moved up to the porch. "Red honey, the boy's got to have a girlfriend someday," said Grankie kindly as I helped her with her chair. "You can't keep him to yourself forever. And you can't choose one for him, either."

"But I'm not!" I tried to explain, but everybody talked over me and laughed at me the way grown folks do when they want to torture kids sometimes. Mom, though, looked at me, smiled a little and shook her head. At least she understood.

To get away from their dumb talk, I headed for the desserts table to get some strawberry pie when *Boom!* In our backyard, right by the food tables, I saw—Anna!

Mom must have, too, because Mom shot down off the porch and over to her. "Hello, may I help you? Looking for someone?" she asked.

"Grankie, that's the one," I heard Taneshia tell everybody. The Tootles came over to Anna, who now wore a black and green shorts and sports bra outfit, with her braids up in a ponytail. She looked like she had stepped off MTV or BET.

"Hey, Jojo; hi, Red." Smiling—but not at me—Anna wiggled her fingers at Jojo and flashed her perfect white teeth. She held out her hand to Mom. "I'm Anna. I live over on Country Club Road and I was just jogging by, and I happened to see Jojo," she said. "Just stopped by to say hey."

"So sure, you sure can. We've been hearing about you," said Mr. Tootle. He was grinning the way that old men do when they see a pretty girl. Miz Tootle wrapped her arm around his and jerked on it. He cut back on his grin. "Jojo, this young lady wants you—I mean, wants to talk to you. You're welcome to stay and have some dinner. Better tell your folks where you are, though. Wanna use the phone?"

Before anybody could say anything, Jojo's dad unhooked himself from his wife, took Anna by the elbow and propelled her over to Jojo. Saying things under her breath, Miz Tootle followed them. We watched the Tootles, Anne and Jojo go into the house. Mom whispered to me, "You know, she *does* seem kinda snaky to me, and in more ways than one. Grankie, wait, let me help you with that."

I scratched my shoulder, my calves, my elbow—I was itching everywhere. I wished I could go over to my house and soak in a bathtub of lotion. I wished I could get a new skin. But I didn't have time to do either. Boyfriend or friend boy, Jojo was still my best friend. I had to see what was going on inside that house.

Miz Tootle and Jojo were in the hallway when I got there. "She's calling her folks on the phone in the can, Red," said Jojo. "I know how you like to keep up with everybody else's business." He walked back toward the porch and slouched up against the screen door with his arms folded.

"Are you and Jojo having a fight?" Miz Tootle asked, then added, "If it's got to do with snakes, don't tell me."

Instead of answering her question, I asked, "Can I have some lotion? I been scratching all day."

Mrs. Tootle nodded and went into her bedroom. Taking a deep breath, I started toward Jojo. I wanted to explain to him that if Anna was the girl he wanted, well, okay, fine with me. No big deal. I suppose I could stand it. Maybe I *was* pressing in on his personal business. Maybe she wasn't a snake. Maybe I just wanted her to be. I was going to tell him that he could have a million girlfriends, and I'd stay out of his way. I was sorry if I'd been nosy. But I still wanted to be his best friend, no matter what.

When I set my mouth to say all this, Miz Tootle let out a whoop louder than the one she gave this afternoon. I jumped around to see her shoot through her bedroom door and slam the door shut. There it was! In the hallway! That same blonde, black and green-patterned *snake*—with the yellow-green eyes! It hissed, "Now it's just you and me, Red. Of course, I marked Jojo! Bet you didn't know that I marked you, too! Now I—look at you! Look at you!"

When I peered at my feet, I couldn't see them. That was because I was lying on the carpet, and I couldn't find my arms to push myself up. In the hallway mirror I saw a long, writhing, red, black and brown scaly snake body looking back at me. It WAS me!

The floor began to thump and vibrate all along my body. With what was left of my human brain, I realized three things: that I had become a snake—again?, that danger was approaching and I better move my long behind out the way of it, and that Anna had disappeared.

As fast as I could wiggle (wiggle!) I undulated into the kitchen, slipped and slid across the slick linoleum floor, and rolled behind the refrigerator. The damp darkness smelled like floor wax, rotten celery and dried-up grapes. I lay among the dust balls and with what was left of my human brain tried to make sense of what had happened. Oddly enough, I felt calm. But whoever heard of a hysterical snake?

I know I hadn't wanted to prove my theory like this—firsthand. The itching must have come from when Anna first touched me. Her touch must have brought my snake life back somehow. From what I had seen of me in the mirror, I was an Eastern milk snake. Again. When I opened my mouth, a long forked tongue flicked out. I could "smell" barbecued chicken and shish kebabs through it.

"No, I don't know where they went! Yes, there were two! Or was it one?" Miz Tootle was screaming. "Anna, you gotta get out of that bathroom now. There's a big snake loose in the house!"

When I slid forward a few inches, the floor disappeared and I landed with a hard thud on the dirt beneath the house. Through the foundation vent I could hear and see my parents, Jojo, the Tootles, Grankie—everybody. And Anna. *She was a girl again*. Well now, if she could be a girl again, couldn't I?

I laid my special look on Jojo until his eyes shifted down toward the foundation vent where I lay. I was sure he was looking right into my eyes. Anna said to the Tootles, "I think you should call the snake exterminator right away," and they were nodding.

Jojo spoke up. "Oh no, you can't do that. You—you just can't. No, I don't know why you can't, Mom, Dad, but—I'll catch it, I promise; I'll put it in our lab, or take it to the Wildlife Shelter, okay?"

If I had had lips I would have smiled. Jojo would have to check the lab before he went to bed tonight. And when he did, I'd be there waiting for him. I'd mark him myself and get back to being Red in no time at all. And if Anna was with him, no problem, I'd mark her, too, for good. We Eastern milk snakes eat other snakes, anyway. I'd love to get my fangs into her. Wait until I write up my *next* theory and turn it in to English class!

At the rustle of something behind me, I turned my

head slightly and flicked out my tongue. The little grass frog from the sprinkling can was frozen in my sight. In an instant I stretched out my body, snatched the frog with my jaws and swallowed it alive. I had always loved frog legs. Now I knew why.

Final Cut

Rich Wallace

I got cut from teams twice in my life: junior football as a twerpy fourth-grader and freshman basketball five years later at Hasbrouck Heights High School in New Jersey. Both times I tried hard to turn it into something positive. Mostly by developing an attitude that wouldn't let it happen again. The kind of attitude that keeps you in the driveway shooting baskets after dark, or at the track running 400-meter intervals long after the rest of the team has packed it in.

Maybe the best thing a coach ever did for me was back in seventh grade, when the basketball coach—Bob Biegel—took me aside and told me why he *wasn't* cutting me. He said something about how I won every wind sprint and went after every loose ball, even though I was clueless about defense and most of my shots hit the side of the backboard. I didn't play in the games much, so I did the team no harm. But it sure did me a lot of good to know that I'd earned the right to be there.

Wednesday night Nicole comes into the Y when I'm shooting baskets, a week or two sooner than I expected. She's very tan from being in Florida, and we say hello and start busting each other's chops like usual.

"Make any yet?" she says as I clank a jumper off the front of the rim.

I smirk at her and show her my fist. She sort of flexes, puts up her dukes.

"You're so butch," I tell her.

She laughs. "Could kick your ass, Bernie," she says.

"Right. You find a job down there?"

She shakes her head. "Didn't even look."

I grab the ball and she covers me tight as I drive, front of her thighs against the back of mine. I pivot and shoot, her hand grazing my wrist. The shot goes in. She smells like powder. She's fluid and firm.

"Make the team?" she asks.

"I'll find out tomorrow," I say.

Over in the corner of the bleachers is this sleazy guy in his twenties she'd been rumored to be seeing, but which she'd vehemently denied when I asked her about it a month or so ago. He's also way tanner than anyone could get in Pennsylvania in November.

I'm no idiot; I can size this up. This guy wouldn't come near the Y for any reason but her.

I've been cut from teams before. Twice.

Fifth grade. Junior football. I weighed fifty-seven pounds, had legs like toothpicks, couldn't catch a pass. But you don't rationalize when you're ten. Getting cut sucked.

Again, in seventh grade, the basketball team. Four-foot-ten. Hustled my butt off and made it to the final day of tryouts. I cried when I got the news. Got out of there in a hurry. Shot two hundred jumpers a day for the next four months.

Back in October rumors were going around that Nicole was seeing this mechanic who had walked out on his wife and their baby and was living above his parents' garage. So when she said she was going south to Tampa and might look for a job, I said I was surprised because I thought she was involved with somebody here. She said no, who? I said it doesn't matter, I just heard something. She goes, tell me. So I do. She laughs and says no way.

I didn't completely buy it, but I figured the denial, plus the trip to Florida, were evidence that she might be rethinking the whole idea. And why would she lie to me unless she was interested?

Nicole was a star. In a town where nobody ever went to girls' basketball games she suddenly had them outdrawing our boys' team. Twenty-six points a game she pumped in last winter; got them to the quarterfinals of the state tournament. Went off to some junior college out by Pittsburgh a week after she barely graduated from Sturbridge High School but was back in town by Independence Day, working in the checkout line at Kmart.

Attitude. She played against guys in the Y league the rest of the summer: humid evenings, blacktop court inside a chain-link fence. I held her to seven points one night. In the rematch she scored thirty, sprinting and teasing and challenging me, muttering "give me the friggin' ball" when a teammate would freeze, igniting the fast break, and dazzling everybody with her drive-to-the-basket frenzy.

Cute as hell, too, if I haven't implied that already.

Others start showing up, and we go three-on-three for a while, half-court. I practically live here at the Y, playing pickup games for two or three hours every evening in this tight, rickety old gym. Even this week, even with the intensity of the tryouts after school, I've been putting in a daily appearance after dinner. It soothes the nerves, takes off some of the pressure. Gets me out of the house.

I'm a senior. A guard on a team that's lousy with guards. A team in transition—this will definitely be a rebuilding year (It always seems to be a rebuilding year in our program.) Coach has implied pretty strongly that he'll be in a youth-oriented mode this season. That does not have positive implications for seniors like me with no varsity experience.

If I get cut I keep playing at the Y, try to get in the

men's league, and go back to working in the kitchen at the diner. If I get cut.

I am not a pessimist, but I am nearly certain my fate was determined before tryouts even started. Coach is not the type to hold a spot for a guy like me, whose only major attributes are energy and speed. You can see him pushing the younger guys, sophomores with three whole seasons yet to develop.

The guy stays there in the bleachers the whole time we play—two frickin' hours—going outside now and then for a cigarette, and Nicole barely acknowledges that he's there. She acts the same as always, never afraid to get physical, never letting up on the chatter. "Little guy," she calls me once. I hate that.

A few months ago there was Cyndi, who I'd see a couple of times a week in the Y's weight room. We'd flirt a lot. She's my age but goes to school over at Wallenpaupack. I heard she had a boyfriend who was a scumbag. I heard they broke up. One day I'm watching her lift weights with her legs—great legs, by the way—and I told her she should start running. She said she didn't know how and she needed somebody to teach her. That was a hint I could follow.

We made plans to meet the next day up at the track, and then we ran together once or twice a week for a couple of weeks. We even hung out on Main Street one drizzly August evening. Then she said she was going to visit a friend down in Philadelphia over Labor Day weekend and she'd call me when she got back. She didn't.

I saw her at the Y a few days later and everything seemed okay. The next time I saw her I asked her out for real. She said the reason she went to Philly was so she could get away and think. What she thought up was that she'd give her boyfriend one more chance because he'd been begging her to. She said we could still run together, because you never know what might happen.

Sure is nice to be kept in reserve like that.

We never ran again. I still see her in the gym and talk to her some. She doesn't seem real happy. Last Monday she asked me what I'd done over the weekend. I told her about driving up to this little Delaware River town in New York—Callicoon, if you're ever in the neighborhood—and hanging out behind a bar. They had a blues band playing and we could hear it plain as day from the street. Cyndi said that's the sort of evening she would really enjoy.

When I was much younger, like three months ago, I would have misread that as another hint.

We quit playing at nine. Nicole swats my back and grins. I shut her down pretty well tonight, and for a while there I couldn't miss. "Nice playing," she says, tucking her sweaty hair behind her ear.

"You too," I say.

"Tomorrow night?"

"Probably. Depends." Depends on what happens tomorrow afternoon.

She walks off the court. The old sleazy guy gets up and joins her, and they leave together.

Liar. But I forgive her.

There are things that are within my control, that with effort and desire I can make happen. I can run 800 meters in under two minutes because I am fast enough and strong enough and not afraid to work my butt off in practice.

I can probably get a B average in every class I'm taking, because I am of moderate intelligence and have a study hall every afternoon.

I can probably get into a college, and can probably get a job that will allow me to pay for it. I can probably even get on their basketball team if I choose some scrawny, isolated community college that's desperate for players.

But I can't control what the coach will do tomorrow,

no matter how well I play or how hard. And I can't make Nicole see me as something other than a basketball opponent.

I can control what I do with my body. I can't do a thing about how others perceive me.

The night is warm and clear and there's a million stars overhead, but it still feels gloomy to me. I walk the darkened streets toward home, over cracked and bumpy sidewalks. People never change in this town. If I had a lifeline out of here, a chance to play ball at some college three hundred miles away, you'd have to tie me up and throw me in the back of a truck to get my butt back in Sturbridge. Talent like that and she's working at Kmart! What the hell was she thinking?

My mother is awake, smoking, watching a black-and-white sitcom rerun from forty years ago. There's no other light in the house.

"Hey," I say.

"Hey yourself."

I walk past, into the kitchen, and turn on the light. "Dad home?" I call back.

"What do you think?"

I don't answer. I fish around in the refrigerator and take out a Coke.

"You get your homework done, Bernie?" she says.

"Yeah."

"You get that room cleaned up?"

"Not yet."

I sit at the kitchen table and glance at the pile of mail. The faucet is dripping steadily into the sink, as it's done ever since I can remember. It's hitting the pile of dishes.

"Did he come home after work?" I finally ask.

"Not tonight," she says.

No surprise there. I finish the Coke, take another look in the refrigerator, and stand in the silence for a minute.

I stick my head into the living room. "Going to bed," I say.

"So go."

Twenty-two of us still in contention. Final day. He'll probably keep eighteen, with ten playing JV and a few of them sitting varsity. My only chance is varsity, of course, and I count at least three guards ahead of me. Plus he's got his eye on this sophomore kid, Lenny.

I tighten my shoes, take the floor. My shooting touch was there yesterday, but it can disappear in a hurry. I take a ball and dribble out by the three-point arc. I drive, pull up for a twelve-footer. It bangs around the rim and falls in.

Ed bounces it back to me. I shoot again and miss. I'm a little light-headed. That's nerves. The nerves will go away as soon as we get started. As soon as I can run and play some defense.

Coach blows his whistle, tells us to line up at both baskets for layups. "Concentrate," he says. "I'm watching. There's not a guy in this gym who's made the team yet."

Gym teacher in his forties. Loves to play up that pressure angle, making believe he doesn't already have his lineup penciled in somewhere. He knows his starters, he knows his men off the bench; hell, he's already got next year's team booked in his head. There are only a few of us on the margin here today. Only a few who will live or die by today's performance.

When I got cut from that football team the coach called us over—about ten kids—and gave us this spiel about not enough uniforms to go around. Screw you, man. Don't patronize me. I went home and made a weight set out of detergent bottles filled with sand.

Thing is, two of those kids went back the next day with

their fathers and wound up on the team. Screw them. Their daddies, too. Earn it if you want it bad enough.

We shoot layups and jumpers and run some line drills and passing. We go through some out-of-bounds plays, work on boxing out and rebounding. Everybody knows we'll be scrimmaging for at least an hour. Everybody knows that'll be decisive.

He lines 'em up. Full-court. The five likely starters against his next five favorites. Lenny's out there with the second five. I take a seat on the bottom row of the bleachers. I take a deep breath. I wait.

Craig Duryea, the only returning starter, is running the offense for the top five, with Lenny guarding him. It's a decent matchup. Craig's stronger, Lenny's taller and lanky. Lenny blocks Craig's first shot, grabs the ball, and fires a pass that leads to a fast-break layup. You can see how his confidence has been growing all week.

I watch the back and forth. Craig's experience and muscle keep them even, but Lenny has his moments. He's got a natural feel for the game, a presence. He's not just a head-banger like I am. Needs patience, needs strength, tends to bring the ball up in front on his cross-over dribble, but you can't deny the potential.

After ten minutes Coach puts me in for Craig. Good sign, maybe, going in with the top group. But it's also a chance to hang myself.

The junior-high basketball coach at least didn't pull any punches when he cut me. Nice guy, glasses, just a year out of Rutgers. "You're kind of small," he told me, "not a great ball-handler. Lot of pep, though. Keep working."

The next year I made it. Eighth, ninth man. Got my minutes. That coach respected me, and likewise.

* * *

I nod to Lenny. He nods back. I have to beat his butt to have any chance of making the team, but he must know he's safe. Worst-case for him is a spot on the junior varsity; worst-case for me is the end of my career.

He brings the ball up. I shadow him, not going for the steal, but not giving up the inside. He passes to the wing, then hangs back. He cuts, I stick. There's a shot that misses. Our center grabs the rebound, finds me. Lenny guards me full-court. I shield the ball and dribble up quickly.

Run the show, I'm telling myself. I'll take the shot if it's there, but I need to be an assist man, to get the ball inside. Use my head.

Instead I look at the rim. I feel a quick wave of heat, like a fever, and give a dart to my right. Lenny lunges and I pull up, firing a line drive that finds the back of the net and falls in.

I trot back. "Nice shot," says Barry Ames, our power forward, whacking my arm. Somebody yells, "Turn," and Lenny is already across the mid-court line, coming strong.

I pick him up, shielding the lane. He finds a man inside, makes a nice pass. They score.

I bring the ball up. Lenny picks me up at the foul line, tries to drive me to the side. Another guy comes over and they trap me, but I get rid of the ball safely and drift inside.

The ball comes back to me. I dribble patiently, send a good bounce pass in to Barry. He gets fouled, makes the shot anyway.

It stays like that. I play hard, don't do anything dumb, hit a couple more jumpers and get a steal or two and some rebounds.

Thirty minutes later I'm drenched. Coach puts Craig back in for me. I get a drink. Sit in the bleachers. Wonder if that was enough.

We finish with free throws, three or four guys at each of the six baskets. I make fourteen out of twenty, look around the gym, and walk off the floor to the locker room.

*   *   *

Three years ago. The freshman team. Just another game. We're down seven with three minutes to play and the coach—my algebra teacher—puts me in when Duryea twists his ankle. I get burned right away, losing my man who makes a pretty quick move for a back-door layup.

We get a basket. They get another. I dribble up-court in a hurry, stop at the top of the key, and let go a three-pointer. It bounces high off the back of the rim, settles on the front, and rolls in.

Teammates make fists at me, guys on the bench holler, "Hustle!" My man feints right, tries to cut left, and I jab a hand in there, knock the ball loose. I grab it, turn quickly, and nail Eddie with the pass of my life. Layup. We're within four.

Tight defense. They shoot and miss. I dribble up again, more confident than I deserve, and shoot another three. No iron at all this time, just that sound of it swishing.

They call time-out. Thirty-four seconds left. One point behind. We're jumping up and down in the huddle; the coach is telling us to relax. "Go for the steal, foul if I say so."

They're choking. We've got a guy trapped in the corner, but all he has to do is dribble out. Instead he shoots, missing everything, and we grab the rebound and start sprinting. To me, to Eddie, there's nothing inside. I take the ball and drive the lane, getting as high as I'm able. I bank this one off the glass. It scores. The buzzer sounds. They mob me.

I want another moment like that one.

I'm standing in front of my locker naked, toweling off from the shower, when Coach comes by and taps me on the shoulder.

"Come in the office for a second after you get dressed," he says.

I shut my eyes. Damn it. Damn it to hell. They make the final cuts in private, giving you some dignity I suppose. Letting you slip out quietly before those who made it start celebrating. I can take it. Goddammit. There are no bitter tears in me.

I blink hard a couple of times, stare into my locker. Then I pull on some socks, my underwear, the rest of my clothes. I look around at the steam from the showers, the younger guys snapping towels at each other, the sign on the wall that says DEFENSE!

The office is spare. A gray desk, a phone, some posters on the wall, a couple of chairs. He leans against the desk. I stand in the doorway.

"Nice effort today," he says, cushioning it. "All week."

"Thanks." I look him in the eye, look down.

"You surprised me, Bernie."

"How?"

"I didn't plan to keep you."

I let out my breath. "I kind of figured that."

"Coaches have to make tough decisions," he says. "Sometimes you have to let a guy go, especially a senior, to make room for somebody with more future. A basketball future, I mean."

"I know." I've seen this before. I expected it. Hell, when I was a sophomore he cut some seniors to keep me.

"I can't do it to you, though," he says, and I feel a sudden jolt. I look him in the eye again.

"I can't promise you many minutes," he says, "but there'd be no justice if I cut you from this team. Be here tomorrow at three."

"You got it." I feel my cheeks flush. My eyes are warm. I wipe them with the back of my hand as I turn to leave the office.

Nine o'clock comes. I've been playing easy tonight, not pressing, not worrying; playing with my head as much as with my body. I'm sweaty, warm, tired. I take a seat in the bleachers.

Nicole comes over and sits next to me as I'm pulling on my sweats. The boyfriend isn't here tonight.

"Heard you made the team," she says.

"Yeah. Somehow."

"Nice going."

I nod my head, bite down on my lip. "Final season."

She stares straight ahead, wipes some sweat off her forehead. "Cherish it," she says. "It goes by in a second."

We're quiet then. There's a three-on-three game going on at one basket and an older guy shooting jumpers at the other.

"What happened?" I say, a question I've been wanting to ask her since summer.

She shrugs. Waits. Shakes her head slowly. "I just wasn't ready," she says. "Not yet. They said they'll take me back next semester if I stay in shape. If I'm ready to leave home. I think I will be . . . I think I will."

We don't say anything else. We just sit there, but it feels right. It feels like we're communicating. Like the conversation hasn't ended.

She gets up, gives me a smile that isn't a challenge or a chop-busting. "Next week?" she asks me.

"Yeah," I say. I'll have practice every day, but I'll get here in the evenings. I'm not ready to leave yet either.

I'm glowing as I walk down the steps of the Y alone, needing some food and some sleep. It's turned wet and cold. I pull my cap down low over my brow as I walk the cracked and bumpy sidewalks toward home. People never change in this town.

It's a beautiful evening. The rain is lashing my face now, the wind blowing harder. This is one of the best days I've had in long, long time.

The best day of my life, so far.

The World of Darkness

Lois Metzger

Some people wonder if they'll ever have anything to write about. I've heard it said that everyone has three great stories to tell. Other people wonder if they can even write at all. "If you can talk," a teacher once told me, "you can write."

Several years ago, I had an experience in the Bronx Zoo that happened almost exactly as it happens in this story, "The World of Darkness." I remember feeling particularly lost that day, but after my visit to the zoo I felt much better—uplifted, even. I found that I was telling people about this experience, how powerful it was in its way. This got me thinking that there might be a story here.

The character of Gail Gruber came later. I wanted to create a girl for whom this experience would have maximum impact. In the story, Gail starts out feeling lost, and ends up feeling . . . maybe not "found," but at least not so lost anymore.

By the way, it's true that if you can talk, you can write. But it's not true about having three great stories to tell.

You have many more.

Gail Gruber felt lost.

I'll end up in the Lost & Found, she thought, *where no one will claim me. I'll turn into a little old lady, sitting there with all the other things that got left behind, jackets and scarves and gloves that don't match—*

". . . you'd think you two were glued together or something." A girl at the next desk was talking to Gail. She had masses of black hair and heavy eyebrows.

"What?"

"You and Trudy. You were like Siamese twins, separated at birth but trying to get attached back together."

"More like bosom buddies," said a guy behind Gail. "But I guess you're both too flat-chested, huh?"

Gail ignored him and turned to the girl. What was her name, anyway? Come to think of it, she couldn't remember the guy's name, either. "Trudy and I aren't friends anymore." There, she'd said it out loud, something she'd only been able to say inside her own head. It was a fact now, fixed and absolute, like in math—one plus negative one equals zero.

"There's an awful lot of talking over there!" Ms. Sklar, the freshman Biology teacher at Belle Heights High School, glared in Gail's direction. But she didn't single anyone out. Maybe she couldn't remember their names, either. "Now, as I was saying, pay close attention to the home environments of your animals." Oh, right. Field trip. They were going to the Bronx Zoo to study . . . what was it? The home environments of animals. "Now, choose a partner for your independent study theme. Sit with your partner on the bus, and discuss your theme, and once we're at the zoo, stay with your partner at all times . . ."

Stay with your partner. Wasn't that what best friends did, stay together? Of course Trudy would have been Gail's partner. It would have happened automatically, without words. Now Gail had to ask this girl. "Be my friend, okay? I mean—partner." What a slip!

"Sure, Gail. Whatever."

Trudy, way over on the other side of the room, had picked some guy to be her partner. Gail couldn't help keeping half an eye on Trudy . . . Trudy the Betrayer. It sounded like a TV show. *Next week, on an all-new "Trudy"—Trudy, the False Friend, the Treacherous Traitor, lets someone else down! Who will it be? Stay tuned for scenes from next week's show!*

* * *

It was one of those sealed-in buses. Despite the fact that it was a perfect spring day, all fluffy clouds and radiant sunshine, the air-conditioning was on full blast and the tinted windows made it look like it would rain buckets. The seats were padded but managed to be stiff and uncomfortable anyway, and the seat belt cut right into Gail's middle. Of course, she wouldn't have noticed or cared with Trudy beside her. The two of them were always in their own world, complete with its own weather system—fluffy clouds and radiant sunshine, despite tinted windows.

Gail's new partner talked nonstop. "Do you think Ms. Sklar is married? She's so tall, six-feet-four, can you believe it? Do you think men like that? Should I wear those shoes, you know, the ones with the four-inch platforms?"

"Maybe," Gail said. This girl smelled like cough medicine. Trudy always smelled like oranges—she had a tiny glass vial of perfume she carried around with her. "So, what aspect of the home environment do you think we should focus on?"

That kept her quiet for a while.

I'm leaving you. Last night's phone conversation with Trudy just came into Gail's head. *I don't love you anymore.*

No, wait, Trudy hadn't actually said that. That was something Gail had overheard a guy telling his girlfriend at a bus stop. Not that it was Gail's fault, eavesdropping. She'd tried not to listen; she couldn't help it. The guy's jaw was tight and firm. The girlfriend, who looked so tired, spoke first: "I'm not feeling so hot. I had spinach salad for lunch. I told the waiter, no bacon, but I think there was bacon in it. Bacon always gives me stomachaches. So what's this big important thing you have to tell me?" It took the guy forever, or so it seemed to Gail, to say, "I don't know, I don't love you anymore, I'm leaving you, I guess that's what I'm trying to say, I don't love you and I'm leaving you." The woman looked him right in the eye. "All right, all right," she said, "you don't have to tell me twice!" He asked if she was okay, and she said she'd already told him—she wasn't feeling so hot, because of the bacon. After he left, she started to cry. Gail wished she could say something—*I know, I heard, I'm so sorry, it's not the bacon, I know.* But overhearing was bad enough.

Last night, Trudy had said she was going off to Asia for tenth and eleventh grade, some kind of "Study Abroad" program. Gail didn't want to hear the details. Of course, Gail knew Trudy had applied, but getting in was one thing, and actually deciding to go was something else.

Gail and Trudy had been best friends since they met, four years before, on the first day of middle school, when their homeroom teacher had placed them side by side, saying, "I'm sure your mother would want you to sit together."

Mother?

Gail and Trudy looked each other over. Both had wavy dark blonde hair to their shoulders, dark green eyes, pale skin with freckles. "What's your name?" they whispered.

Gail Gruber.

Trudy Garber.

It was too funny!

"Nice to meet you, identical twin sister," Trudy said. "Where've you been hiding all my life, in the attic? Come to think of it—" she pretended to be shocked, "I don't have an attic!"

Gail laughed. Amazingly, too, their birthdays were only a week apart.

After that, Gail and Trudy saw each other every day, or at least spoke on the phone. They both cried when Trudy broke up with that guy in seventh grade; and also when that guy's cousin dumped Gail. Trudy barely left

Gail's side after Gail broke her leg and had to use crutches for six weeks, and Gail helped Trudy pass algebra—with a B, even.

"You girls never fight," Gail's mother once remarked. "But when you do—watch out!"

"But, Mom," Gail said, "if we *never* fight—"

"You know very well what I mean. It's such a rare thing. But then there's yelling and tears, and you don't know which end is up, and then you make up, and there's even more tears. You're the two most emotional girls I've ever known."

"We are *not* emotional!" Gail covered her ears.

On the phone, Trudy had pleaded, "It's an adventure, can't you see that?"

"How can it be an adventure, without me? How can you just go off, so far away—" Gail had practically never even left Queens. There'd never been a question about her finishing high school right here. How did Trudy get so . . . adventurous?

"If you were really my friend, you'd want me to go."

"If you were really my friend, you'd stay here with me!"

More things were said, but Gail couldn't—didn't want to—remember them.

"Oh, look, can you believe it, I forgot to buckle up!" The girl next to Gail laughed. "What if we had a crash? Pretty funny, don't you think?"

Was this what life was going to be like now? Talking to people who expected you to laugh when something wasn't funny? Gail and Trudy had the same sense of humor, but exactly. One time, Gail was eating a chicken sandwich in a coffee shop. Two women sat at the next table. Gail, trying not to listen, couldn't help listening. One woman said to the other, "I'm such a nervous wreck, I should be in solitary." The other one said, "You—what about me? What about *my* nerves? I should be there with you!" Trudy found this hilarious. It became a thing they said to each other.

I should be in solitary!
I should be there with you!
Gail pressed her ear flat against the cold window.

Off the bus, the six-foot-four-inch Ms. Sklar assigned groups of kids to different parts of the zoo. *The World of Darkness.* That was where Gail and her partner and several other kids were going. It sounded absolutely right to Gail. That was her world now, the world of darkness. Behind her, Gail heard whispering.

"I'm scared of the dark!"

"Don't worry—I'll protect you."

"Get your hands *off* me!"

Each group had its own guide, a young man or woman all in army-green with THE BRONX ZOO stitched on the sleeves of their shirts. Out of the edges of her vision Gail saw that Trudy was in the Wild Asia group. Some other kids were complaining loudly that they didn't want to go on a special, behind-the-scenes tour of the Reptile House. They got assurances that nobody got bitten by snakes or anything like that.

Trees rustled in the cool breeze. Gail heard the distant roar of lions. If she closed her eyes, she could be in some far-off land, on the other side of oceans and beyond deserts and mountains . . .

Gail opened her eyes. "Wild Asia" was the closest she'd ever get to the real Asia.

". . . there'll be a test on home environments," Ms. Sklar was saying.

If Trudy were Gail's partner, she'd come up with some great questions. *Which requires a larger habitat, a rabbit or a rhino?* and *If a person weighing one hundred and twenty pounds visited an adult male lion in his den, how long would it take for that person to get eaten? Show your work.*

The guide for Gail's group was a red-haired woman named Stacey—or was it Nancy? As they walked to the

World of Darkness, which was halfway across the zoo, Gail only caught pieces of what she was saying. "... antelopes, see? They look like deer painted with thin white lines. Keep your eye out for peacocks ..."

Gail heard a child scream. She spun around—only to hear a woman tell her daughter, "All right, already, I'll buy it!" The girl was clutching a stuffed panda.

They passed an open forest called Wolf Wood. Several wolves chased each other around a log. They looked like German shepherds, only bigger, with longer legs and pointier faces.

"Be happy for me," Trudy had said last night. That conversation wouldn't leave Gail alone. "I'd be happy for you."

"Well, that's the difference between us," Gail said. "You're not me."

The World of Darkness was built of dark concrete slabs standing on end, like pieces of a road leading up to the sky. Inside, Gail stood in a small space with a wall of stained glass—a kind of halfway place between darkness and light.

"... the home of nocturnal animals," the guide was saying. Something about animals who sleep all day and stay up at night. Gail knew there'd be a test, so she forced herself to listen more carefully. "We darken the exhibit during the day, so the animals think it's night—that way they're awake when visitors are here. Then we flood the place with light at night, so the animals can get some sleep. Let your eyes adjust to this darkness. When you feel ready, walk around slowly." Gail's partner stood very still, hands cupped over her eyes.

Ready or not, Gail hurried on ahead. All the exhibits were along the walls, behind extra-thick glass—even so, there was a heavy smell of wet fur. Near the snowy owl, Gail saw a tiny sweater on a rail. She could almost hear a voice demanding, *Where's your sweater! Didn't I tell you to keep it on? Now it's lost! Lost forever!* Gail figured she'd overheard so many conversations that now she was overhearing an imaginary one.

On a tree branch sat a slow loris, a furry creature with enormous eyes. It really was slow, with tiny feet moving sluggishly across the branch. Gail wished she could take it home as a pet. "Slow Pokey." That was a good name. The slow loris hung upside down, dangling by its feet, and lifted its head to look right at her. "What is it—*what?*" was its exact expression.

Trudy would have adored that. She would have said a bunch of funny things, too. Trudy could always make Gail laugh. As for Gail, she could always make Trudy . . . what? Maybe that was the problem. Maybe that was why Trudy was going away, and Gail was staying here. *Here*, without Trudy. Gail felt the loss like an ache all over her body.

She came to a huge display—the Cave of Bats. It looked like there were thousands of them, flying in huge sweeps through caverns and over a pond. There must have been a microphone somewhere inside the exhibit, because Gail could hear the amplified sounds of bat squeaks and wings fluttering. It was all so lush and mysterious, it nearly hypnotized her. *This is my home environment*, said a different voice that came into Gail's head.

"I'll bet you're scared to death."

Gail shivered. Who would say such a thing? She turned to see a man with spiky hair like porcupine quills, talking to a small, thin boy who wore a Yankees cap. The boy was maybe five years old, and the man was poking him in the shoulder. "You didn't know bats were so ugly, did you?"

"I don't think they're ugly," the boy said quietly.

Gail noticed a sign overhead, telling people to talk softly, but this man spoke at full volume. "Hey, maybe they can break out of there, did you think of that? What if they flew in your hair? You'd have to get your head shaved! We could call you Baldy! Baldy McBaldy, how's that?"

The boy didn't say anything, only stared straight ahead without blinking.

Suddenly one of the bats hit the glass hard. Then it fell into the pond.

"It'll drown!" the boy cried out.

"Don't be ridiculous. Don't you think bats know what they're doing? It was only trying to get out, to bite you on the neck—"

"It's drowning, Daddy, it's drowning! Look!"

"I'm looking. Now why would they put a pond in there if bats didn't know how to swim?"

Was the bat swimming? It was kind of . . . flapping around. Was it scared? Alone, even among thousands of bats? Gail wanted to say something to this man, but of course she wouldn't. Overhearing was one thing; interfering was something else.

What would Trudy do? Something, of course. Trudy would stop people on the street to give them directions. *How did you know they needed help?* Gail would ask. *They looked lost*, Trudy would say. If people looked lost to Gail, she would walk by them as if she herself were lost.

What would Trudy do?

But Trudy wasn't here.

"Excuse me," Gail heard herself saying to the man, "he's right. The bat—it's drowning."

The man looked at her. In the dark, she couldn't tell the color of his eyes, only their intensity. "Who died and made you keeper of the bats?"

"Nobody." Gail became suddenly aware of her own body, the weight of it, how it took up space and got held there by gravity. "Look, it's fighting to keep its head up—"

"You *must* be the keeper of the bats, then!"

Keeper of the Bats. All right. That's me. Not Trudy. Me. Gail hurried to find the guide, and found her over by Slow Pokey. "Listen, there's a bat—it hit the glass and now it's in the water, struggling—"

Instantly the woman ran to the exhibit. She opened a door that had been invisible, camouflaged somehow, and was suddenly, magically, inside the Cave of Bats. She lifted the bat out of the pond with both hands and held it for a moment. It shook itself off, the way dogs do. Then she hung it upside down on a tree—and quickly disappeared through the hidden door.

"See, Daddy, it was drowning!"

"It must've been a young bat," the man grumbled. "The older ones are expert swimmers."

Gail shook her head. There was nothing she, or anyone else, could do. This boy was stuck with it.

"Hey, thanks!" The woman ran over to Gail. "You saved a life!"

"So it was really dying?"

She spoke loud enough for the boy and his father to hear. "Maybe it could've pulled itself to safety, but maybe not. This little one was having a really rough time. See, when some bats get wet they can't fly. The big ones, the ones with wingspans of five feet, can fly around and get dry. But when they're little, we have to hang them up to dry—like laundry!"

"So it was frightened, right? But not anymore."

The woman smiled. Her smile was relaxed and open. "No, not anymore."

"So . . . what's your name, again?" Gail tried to start a real conversation, the way Trudy would.

"Stephanie."

"I'm Gail. I just remembered something. When you're drowning, you're supposed to look for bubbles. Bubbles always float to the surface, so that way you know which way is up. I mean, not that bats can remember that kind of thing."

"No, but it's good for us human beings to remember!"

There was something else, too. "Is there a Lost &

Found? Somebody lost a sweater, over by the snowy owl—"

Stephanie said she'd take care of it.

Before leaving the World of Darkness, Gail stopped in front of a display called THE MOST DANGEROUS ANIMAL IN THE WORLD. It was a mirror, just as she knew it would be, and there were bars in front of the mirror. She stared at her own caged reflection.

Outside, Gail blinked hard. She figured she'd wait there for her partner. Who knows? Maybe the girl was looking for her. The man with the spiky hair was outside, too, smoking a cigarette. He stood in the shadow of the World of Darkness, which Gail imagined must be the darkest place of all.

The little boy ran up to a woman who was also smoking. "Mommy, Mommy! We saw a bat plop in the water, and a lady had to come and rescue it."

"I don't want to hear about bats." The woman took another drag. "Why do you think I didn't go in in the first place?"

"But it was drowning, and Daddy said it wasn't—"

"*Enough*," the man said. "If you love the bats so much, I'll take you back and leave you there!"

"Frankly," the woman said, "that place gives me the creeps. It looks like a prison. You'd think they'd put in some windows."

The man glanced at Gail. She could tell he didn't recognize her. The boy glanced over, too. He knew her, even in the light. He squirmed and grabbed his father's leg.

The sun was low in the sky and Gail felt cool air on her face. She'd been wrong, and now she knew it. Of course Trudy should go away. Gail could even be happy for her, in time. When she saw Trudy at the bus, she would tell her. She would tell her about the drowning bat, and Baldy McBaldy, and ask about Wild Asia, and Trudy would say something funny, of course, something about how she really thought she was in Asia, not the

Bronx, and how did they do that, it was so convincing, and what a shock, to come back and find herself *here*—

Trudy would be going away, but she was here for now, and for the rest of the school year, and for summer. And when Trudy left, Gail would be able to hear Trudy's voice in her head, the things she might say. That was kind of like having Trudy's company. Gail would write to her, too. Gail, Keeper of the Bats.

Some people, like Trudy, were born brave, or maybe it only seemed that way, and others had to work at it.

A Safe Space

Joyce Hansen

This story was inspired by two students I met several years ago in a junior high school in a small midwestern city. I was there to conduct a writing workshop for about thirty students in the school library. I noticed two young men who sat at the same table, wrote together and appeared to be good friends. Both of them were excellent writers. One of them was black and the other one was white. The school was predominantly African American—including the principal and her staff. I sensed that the white student was very comfortable with himself and his classmates.

Later on that day, when I was speaking with a group of teachers about the students, they told me that the white student was in fact very comfortable and fit in well with his peers. They related that he'd even joined the gospel choir and when the choir performed, a student stood on either side of him and swayed him so that he'd move in time to the music, along with the rest of the choir.

I was amused, fascinated and then impressed by this story, and these students. What a fine example of cooperation, acceptance and inclusion among young people, who are so often accused of being intolerant of those who are different from themselves.

The characterizations and events in this story are all fictional. I tried to deal with issues that touch young lives. However, the spirit of caring and understanding that I hope this story conveys comes from the wonderful young people I met that day.

Concentrate! Only one hour before showtime, people," Mr. Walker yells. "You're out of sync, son. Stand still. Don't move." A few people giggle. We know who he's shouting at as he taps his baton on the podium.

Poor Tommy. His voice wasn't bad, deep bass like mine. But he couldn't move in time to the music. I knew he shouldn't have joined our high school gospel chorus. I tried to talk him out of it. But like my girlfriend Deidre always says, "Tommy's been around us so long he don't know he's white anymore."

Walker is springing up and down and waving his arms. Tommy stands next to me and I feel him twitch when the altos and sopranos begin to sing "I'll Fly Away," his favorite. And I know that by the time the tenors and the bass join in he will move even though Walker told him not to because Tommy is a feeling person. And the music moves you. It was just that Tommy didn't move the way the rest of us did. For some of our songs we sway from side to side as we sing. Walker is a perfectionist. I call him Perfect Pitch. "We move as one body. We sing with one voice, people," he'd shout at us.

It's our turn. As the tenors and bass sing I can't look at Tommy and he can't keep still. If I look at him I'll get out of whack too. "Concentrate," Walker shouted again. "We move as one body." I wish I could help Tommy.

"*I'll fly away oh glory, I'll fly away.*" Tommy sings with all of his heart. Happy. He breaks loose and moves to his own time. Doesn't care what anyone thinks. Not like me. I've tried to be like Tommy. Not caring. It doesn't work for me. But Tommy never worries about what people think of him. He's been that way ever since I first met him.

The first thing I noticed about Tommy when he walked into the auditorium at freshman orientation two years ago was his large round face and dirty blond hair that wouldn't settle down on his head. *Moonface*. The fact that he was the only white student in the entire ninth grade made him stand out even more—like a big white sore thumb.

I stand out too, but for different reasons—people who like me, mostly my family, call me a "big husky guy." Everyone else, especially my peers, call me *Fat Boy*. At least my size keeps people away from me until they learn that I'm not a fighter. I am just a boy who likes to stay to himself.

On freshman day as I watched kids streaming into the auditorium I scanned the room for a familiar face from my old junior high school—not that it mattered. I had no real friends in junior high school anyway. Instead of seeing a familiar face, I saw Tommy, a very new face. I figured that he wouldn't last a week, and wondered why he was attending Lincoln High School. There were only a handful of white students in the school and they were all seniors. My mom called them the remnants—the families who never left the neighborhood once it changed. "Too poor to leave." She knows everything. I wonder whether she knows why my father left us.

Ninth graders continued to drift into the auditorium and I saw a few familiar faces from junior high school. It didn't take me long to guess who was who and what was what. The boys checked out the girls, except for some of the boys who eyed each other.

The athletes were tall, loud and handsome. Then there were the boys who weren't athletes and they weren't handsome either, but the girls liked them anyway. They knew how to tease girls and put their arms around them without getting slapped upside the head, and they knew how to walk down the hall sideways and make girls laugh. I love girls too, but I am not what the old folks call "a ladies' man."

And there were the boys like me—closet brainiacs. I tried to see if I could recognize any more of us. It was hard, though, because we hide. Some of us hide behind silly grins and others behind bad attitudes. And some, like me, try to disappear completely.

I checked out the girls next. A few of them looked shy and mousy and seemed like they were afraid. Others were boisterous as hell, acting like they were still in junior high school. Next I checked out the fly, pretty girls who God made just for the athletes. Then there was one girl who stood out from the rest. *The Most Popular Girl in the World.*

I noticed her only because she seemed to know everyone. She was thin, small and dark and wasn't much to write home about, I thought, mostly because she was easy to miss in a crowd of athletes and fly girls.

I don't think any of us noticed too much after we left the auditorium, because as soon as we entered the hallway where the real jocks and players ruled, we were little no-count turds and nerds who didn't matter in the great scheme of things. We spun in a whirlwind of students, noise and confusion. Someone yelled get those toddlers. A freshman day ritual.

Me, *Moonface* and *The Most Popular Girl in the World* bumped into one another as we tried to find our way among the stampeding students.

"Hey, I'm sorry man." Moonface ran into me. "You know where room 211 is?"

"I'm near you, room 212," a girl's voice answered.

I turned around and saw *The Most Popular Girl in the World.* I towered over her.

"I'm in room 218," I said, staring at my program. The girl's smile dazzled me, so I looked away.

She put out her hand, "My name is Deidre."

"I'm Lamont," I said.

Moonface held out his hand. "I'm Tommy."

We found our rooms together, but I didn't see them for the next two weeks. I guessed that *The Most Popular Girl in the World* was too busy with all of the people she knew, and that *Moonface* probably had transferred to the predominantly white high school on the other side of town. I was busy surviving. You could survive if you knew how. You had to do things like eat lunch quickly in a quiet corner of the cafeteria, if there was one, and then escape to the library. Instead of riding the school bus or the public buses that many of the kids used, I walked the ten blocks to my house—taking the short cut through Garvey Park.

By the second week of school everyone was settling into their places and we could sign up for extracurricular activities. Nothing interested me, but my mother bugged me about joining a school club. One morning before I left for school, we had one of our usual arguments.

"You need to join a club in your school. You spend too much time alone, Lamont."

"I like to be alone," I said, knowing that this would bring on the "Black People Are Not Loners" speech. "It's unnatural, especially for a black person. Most black people are social."

"But I'm not most black people," I said. "How do you know how most black people are, anyway?" I asked, knowing that this would bring on the "You Are Just Like Your Father" speech. I left the house before she dipped into her bag of speeches and pulled out another one.

Why couldn't she understand that being a loner wasn't such a terrible thing? Especially when you liked to write poetry. But no one knew this about me—not even my mother, or my father when he lived with us. He probably would've said that writing poetry wasn't a very manly thing to do. In his world only athletes were manly. So, I joined the writing club. Sitting quietly in a corner and writing sounded good to me. I'd stay long enough to keep my Moms quiet, then I'd go back to being my unnatural self.

When I walked into the classroom for the first meeting, who do I see but *Moonface* and *The Most Popular Girl in the World.* Deidre and Tommy sat together at a large round table. They both grinned and motioned me over to them. They acted like they'd been waiting for me. I had no choice but to sit with them.

I was annoyed, though. I figured Tommy just wanted to goof off or he was afraid of the general population and thought that the kids in the creative writing club wouldn't harrass him. And I figured Deidre liked some boy in the club, though there were not too many of us except for a table full of the guys who knew how to make girls laugh and an athlete who must've been hiding out from the real thugs who were majoring in gangsterism 101 and wanted to kick his ass.

Mrs. Mackey, the teacher who ran the club, reminded me of a hippie back in the sixties. Old and young at the same time.

"All of you have something important to say. Search your own hearts and minds. Everything you need to create is right here." She placed her hand on her heart. "No one is wrong here. We're exploring and creating together."

Then we did what she called a freewriting exercise. "Don't edit yourself. Be free. What you have to say is important because you're important. Find the quiet place, the safe space inside of you. There has to be a place where you find peace, love and freedom from your fears. You have to find a safe space that allows you to be strong and to soar." Her voice rose. "Write, don't stop. You can't be wrong or sound stupid." Her silver earrings danced and dangled around the sides of her face as she talked. "Believe in yourself. Trust your voice, your heart."

Tommy pulled a big looseleaf notebook out of his backpack like it was special for the occasion. And he began to write and I wondered why he wrote so fast and furiously. I didn't know what to write. As a matter of fact, I thought that the whole exercise was stupid. Write anything that comes to your mind? Mrs. Hippie had talked about a safe space.

Mama, Papa
Once a safe space in
a boy's life. When did it start?
Muffled sounds in the night.
Cries you can't hide.
The hate seeping into the cracks of the walls
oozing out of ceilings sliding under doors.

I stopped, even though she said to keep writing. I glanced at Tommy, who had written two full pages. Deidre had either drawn something, or created her own alphabet.

"Now I want us to share," Mrs. Mackey said after ten minutes, "but only if you wish to."

Everyone looked everywhere but at the teacher. No one wanted to stand up and read the crap they'd written. Then Tommy raised his big white hand. *Why*? I thought. *Why would you open yourself to ridicule?*

Tommy cleared his throat and I heard some snickers. They're going to make chicken liver out of this kid I thought to myself. He began to read and Mrs. Hippie's face grew long and stern as she gazed around the room. Giggles grew like humming insects on a hot summer day. But Tommy kept reading. He read some kind of sci fi story about an alien on another planet, and I wondered was he writing about himself and us? Suddenly the snickering stopped and we all listened to his wild story of lost worlds. This kid has seen one Star Trek episode too many, I said to myself.

But when he stopped reading just before his character is about to be crushed by a crazed robot, and announced, "I didn't finish yet," everyone groaned.

Then the athletic-looking kid says to Tommy in a deep voice that could be considered threatening if you were the scary type, "Man, don't leave me hanging like that. Finish the story the next time."

Deidre laughed and it sounded like a song. "I'll help you finish the story," she offered. "I have some ideas." Then she turned to me. "What did you write?"

"Nothing," I said.

Her smile brushed my face, like soft hands. "I bet you're a real good writer, Lamont."

I let her read it. "Don't show anyone else," I said. I don't even know what made me show her. Her smile, I suppose. I had never let anyone read my poetry except a few teachers who promised not to make me read before the class.

Tommy leaned over Deidre's shoulder. "Can I read it too?"

I figured if he had the nerve to stand up in front of us like that, then I could let him read what I'd written. It was just an exercise, anyhow. But that was the beginning of our friendship. The three of us became best buddies and Deidre ended up being my girl.

Deidre wasn't *The Most Popular Girl in the World.* That was her way of surviving and keeping people off guard. Making them think that they knew her—always helpful. She's a brainiac too. She knew she couldn't fit in with the cheerleaders, or the fly girls, and the mousy girls were boring. She really wanted to be in a math club, but Lincoln High School has no math club. So she joined the writing club, and decided to stay because she liked me. (Is the girl crazy?) She never had a boyfriend and confessed to me that most boys frightened her.

Tommy turned out to be a brainiac too. He survived so well he doesn't stand out anymore and refused to go to the white school when his father wanted to transfer him out of Lincoln. He is totally and completely unself-conscious. Impervious to ridicule. Determined to fit in. And he does. He's not the big white kid anymore, but merely Tommy.

Our writing group shrunk. Those of us who stayed really like Mrs. Mackey, even me, who isn't easy to please. She's one of the few adults I ever met who treated you like a person and not a lump of clay to change and mold in their image. The athlete remained—said he wanted to hear the end of Tommy's story. Tommy said he was creating a sci fi soap opera. And Mrs. Mackey said that a story isn't finished until it's finished. And she'd tell Deidre that it was okay to visualize her stories through drawing. She let the boys who knew how to make girls laugh create rapping, rhyming stories. And she accepted me.

"I wish you would share what you write with the other students, Lamont. It would help them, because I know that they have the same feelings. You have so much talent." Then she'd smile. "But I understand if you don't wish to read before the group." The other day I showed her "A Safe Space." I keep fooling around with it. Adding things, taking things away. I showed her a few lines that I'd added to it.

You know everything,
yet couldn't make him stay?
And You. Did you have to leave?
Do you detest the sight of me and her?
Is that why you hide?
But you filled the house and
made it a home too.

Mrs. Mackey clasped her hands to her chest and almost looked teary-eyed. "You have a poet's soul. This is so moving."

"I'm not finished with it," I said. And left it at that.

Each time I went to the club I promised myself that I'd read in front of the class. As I tried to raise my head and my hand I'd break out in a cold sweat, then I'd feel like I was blowing up like a helium balloon. I couldn't do it.

I write stories and plays too, and I've come up with some pretty good rhymes also, but my deepest feelings can only be expressed in a poem. Mrs. Mackey always shows us different forms of writing, so we'd try new things.

I still only share what I write with Mrs. Mackey, Tommy and Deidre. Deidre has offered to read my poems to the rest of the group, but I won't let her. I joined the gospel chorus because I thought it would help me. But it's not the same as me standing alone. In the chorus, I am one of thirty people.

I feel so ridiculous because I still can't bear to hear my words read aloud. Yet, last week I did something real crazy. Mrs. Mackey is always telling me how moving my words are. Pumping me up. My mother had been bugging me all last week, telling me to let my father know about the concert. "Did you tell *your father* about the concert?"

"Yes."

"What did he say?"

"I don't know what he said."

"You act just like *your father.*" She shook her head. "You can't go through life sticking to yourself like that. You can't talk to your own father? It ain't natural."

I played with her words:

She misses you, but never speaks your name,
or tells me why you left us alone.
Your name is now, "Your Father."
Your Father hasn't called.
Your Father isn't here.
Your Father doesn't care.
You act just like Your Father.

I didn't answer her because I don't think she wanted an answer. I wonder what she would say if she knew I sent him "A Safe Space" along with a note: *I'll be singing at a concert in the high school auditorium on Wednesday night at 7:30. Lamont.*

I'm wondering how I had the nerve to do that? Anger? Maybe. Spite? Maybe. If my poetry is so moving perhaps it will move him to show up at the concert tonight.

As I stand with the others and watch people strolling into the auditorium I begin to feel nervous. Then I feel anger creeping up in me as I see more and more parents, especially fathers. He won't come and he'll call me a big sissy for sitting around writing poems instead of getting my fat ass out on a football field. I let Mrs. Mackey turn my head. I let her pump me up for two years and ended up doing a stupid thing like sending a poem to my father. A man of few words. I can't believe I did that.

Mr. Walker bangs the baton startling me. "People, the time is drawing nigh. Get it together, Mr. Tommy, I told you not to move. Concentrate."

Tommy wipes his forehead. "But, Mr. Walker, I didn't know I was moving."

He pulls Tommy to the side and talks with him privately, so we take a break.

Deidre walks over to me. "Lamont, we have to help him."

I have my own problems. "How? Give him rhythm? I told him not to join the gospel chorus."

"But he likes it. Walker should give him a break."

"Some things you can't help people do. It's impossible," I said. *Just like you and Tommy can't help me to stand up before the writing club.*

Tommy walks over to us and his round face is sagging.

"What did Walker say?" I ask.

"He'd pull me out if I don't keep still." I feel sorry for him. His father and mother walk in. It would be embarrassing if he got thrown out of the chorus while his parents are watching.

My father is nowhere in sight.

"I have an idea, but I have to ask Mr. Walker," Deidre says suddenly and runs over to him. Walker's face stretches into a long frown as he nods impatiently and throws his hands up in the air like he's so frustrated he'd agree to anything.

Deidre dashes back over to me, her face a dazzling smile. "Walker said I could stand on the other side of Tommy and you and I sway him in the right direction when he goes off."

"Walker's letting you sing in the boys' section?"

"It doesn't matter. I know my part. I'll sing when the sopranos do."

"Dee, this ain't gonna work."

"Trust me."

"Why do you always have to be so helpful? We're gonna look like Big Black, Big White and the Little Spasm."

Deidre throws her head back and laughs. Any other girl would get angry.

The audience is full and Walker springs up to the podium like he's on a pogo stick. I start to sweat when I see my mother walk in. She'll have plenty to say—especially about Tommy swaying in the wrong direction. I take a last look around for my father and decide to forget it. I hope the note and the poem got lost in the mail.

We sing "Oh Happy Day," then we belt out "Joy, Joy," and if Tommy even twitches Deidre pulls his robe. He's motionless. We don't sway in those, just a slight rocking back and forth. "I'll Fly Away" is next and my heart beat speeds up. Thanks to Deidre we'll end up looking like three jerks.

He doesn't move for the first few bars, but when we sing "I'll fly away, oh glory, I'll fly away," I feel him twitch and I peek over at him. His eyes are closed, his head thrown back. He's getting ready to break out. Deidre grabs his arm and pulls him in her direction and I grab his other arm. We sway and rock him through the song. The boy has heart.

Suddenly the audience starts to clap and sing along with us. I see Deidre's little head bobbing on the other side of Tommy as she pulls him toward her. The place is rocking and as long as me and Deidre sway Tommy in the right direction, he's moving in time to the music. Walker indicates for us to take another chorus, and Deidre must have gotten some kind of spirit because she lets Tommy go, starts clapping faster and Tommy jerks away from me and claps in his own time making herky-jerky movements. Walker is smiling and bouncing up and down. Doesn't he see Tommy? I guess all of us are swept up by the smiling, clapping, singing audience.

Tommy is all smiles when the concert ends and everyone compliments us. Mr. Walker is all smiles too. He says privately to me and Deidre while Tommy is shaking hands, "Thank you, Mr. Lamont and Miss Deidre. That was a touch of genius." Walker hadn't even seen Tommy going off in his own direction. Perhaps it didn't matter. People see what they want to see in the end.

My mother is running her mouth to a group of parents and she's pointing in my direction. I don't have to hear her to know exactly what she's saying. "That's my son over there. He's a wonderful singer." I see Mrs. Mackey, but I don't want to speak to her now. I'm not blaming her or anything like that for making me send the poem to my father, but I don't want her gushing over me. I also see Deidre heading for the door with her mother and I follow them so that I can tell Deidre good night. When I push open the door I'm shocked.

My father is standing there in his dusty blue pants and shirt, looking confused, like he doesn't know what to do with himself. "Lamont, I'm sorry I missed the concert. I couldn't get away from the garage in time. I heard the last song. I hear you, son. You know what I mean?" He shrugged his shoulders and looked at me kind of pitiful. Like I said, he is a man of few words.

I thought Mrs. Mackey would faint when I raised my hand. I felt the sweaty beads popping out on my forehead, but I was determined this time. Tommy gave me the thumbs-up sign and a few words of wisdom. "When people make you nervous, just think they go to the bathroom same as you do."

Deidre's dazzling smile dried up some of the sweat on my forehead. I walked slowly to the front of the room and reminded myself that my words, perhaps, got my father to show up even if he missed the concert. And even if my mother said, "Just showing up after everything is over isn't good enough."

The other kids laughed and teased as I knew they would, but it was the kind of teasing that friends do to each other. "I don't believe it," one of the rappers said. "It took two years for you to get up here in front of us?"

The athlete shouted, "Man, sit your big self down, don't nobody want to hear what you have have to say now."

I knew that they would goof on me. I deserved it for being afraid to show myself. I felt the sweat popping out again and thought about Tommy swinging to his own time and no one noticing him, because Tommy didn't notice. I smiled at *The Most Popular Girl in the World* and *Moonface*. Though they remained in their seats, it was like they stood on either side of me. Helping me to sway and not feel like a hulk who wanted to break into little pieces. I'd start from the beginning. After I went home the night of the concert, I'd finished "A Safe Space." As I read I began to feel so comfortable in the unnaturalness of me.

Mama, Papa
Once a safe space in
a boy's life. When did it start?
Muffled sounds in the night
Cries you couldn't hide
Hate seeping through
the cracks in the walls
oozing out of ceilings
sliding under doors.
You know everything, yet you
couldn't make him stay?
And you
Did you have to leave?
Do you detest the sight of me and her?
Is that why you hid behind newspapers and
in front of televisions?
She misses you too, but never speaks your name,
or tells me why you left us.
Alone.
Your name is now "Your Father."

"Your Father hasn't called."
"Your Father isn't here."
"Your Father doesn't care—
You act just like Your Father."

But I am me, not really alone.

I have found
A Safe Space of my own.

Sproing!

Joan Abelove

When I first went to college, many years ago, I didn't know anybody and the girl I had corresponded with over the summer who was supposed to be my roommate and who I really liked got moved to another dorm and I felt desperately alone. Like Naomi, I had never had to go and make a friend. I had grown up and gone to school my whole life with the same kids. They were my friends, as God-given as my family.

To compound the problem, I was very shy. The Florida memory in Sproing is also true. I really had no experience meeting new people and I didn't have a clue as to how to go about it. I spent a longer time than Naomi, holed up, scared and lonely, doing homework and reading. I have no idea what I read. I don't think I even knew what I was reading while I read it. And then, like Naomi, I made that big decision—get out and make a friend. The friend I chose was Ruth, who did sit next to me in my freshman English class and was an artist but didn't draw naked people in class. I did what Naomi did, I walked up to Ruth's room and knocked on her door. I am still impressed that inexperienced as I was at choosing friends, I picked a wonderful one. We became and remained very close friends all through college.

That is the first time I ever remember being crystal clear about what I needed and then taking the steps necessary to get it, out of character as those steps were. I always think of that experience as my own version of necessity being the mother of invention.

I am losing it. I have not heard a word since I sat down in this class. Try and pay attention, Naomi. Just try. It'll be better if you listen to something besides your own mind. Pick up your pen. Concentrate, for God's sake. Bless you, Ms. Rosenberg, for speaking slowly. "Footnotes. You will learn the proper way of annotating." Bless you for lecturing and not asking questions. Write down everything she is saying. I may be starting in the middle of a sentence, but at least I can write down every word. Take dictation. You're good at that. "You will learn to use the New York Public Library." Maybe at the end of today, I can read over what she said, try and make sense out of it. No! Listen to it now! Listen to it as it is said.

How am I going to make it through four years like this? I have very good hand-mind coordination. My hand can do whatever it wants, while my mind goes someplace else completely. "Research. Writing a research paper." I can't pat my head with one hand and rub my tummy with the other, but this is better.

It isn't that I'm not a good student. It's that this is my first time in college—say that again, My First Time In College—and I don't know a soul. So I just have my own weird mind to have conversations with. Two weeks—a whole two weeks of conversations only with myself. I can't take it much more.

I do have a roommate—Stacy Upson—I call her Upchuck in my mind—but I can't talk to her. Well, I can talk, I can say, "Hi, how's it going?" and "Have a good day" and stuff like that, but I can't say, "God, aren't you scared shitless? You don't know anyone here either. I am so lonely I could scream. And I am probably the shiest person you will ever meet. Well, maybe not. Maybe there is someone even shier than I am—someone so shy, she lives in a hole in a tree and only speaks to squirrels.

"I grew up in the town where I was born. I went from kindergarten through high school with the same kids. I went to the same sleepover camp for seven years, with my two best friends from home. I have no experience with meeting strangers on my own. HELP!"

But I could say none of this to Stacy, perfect Stacy.

I knew the minute I saw her that I hated her. My Sproing told me. You know, that thing that goes off in your mind when you first meet someone and you don't really think it, it's more like you feel—Sproing! I hate her! Or, Sproing! I like her!

"Hi, my name is Stacy, with a Y." She had reached out to shake my hand as I had entered the room we were supposed to share.

"What's with a Y?" I took her hand. Yuck, what a wimpy grip. If I had a grip like that, I would never offer anyone my hand.

"My name," she said and smiled, condescendingly. That was the only way she ever smiled. She took a beat, then looked down her nose at me, even though I had five inches on her, easy.

What was she talking about?

"You spell my name, Stacy, with a Y."

"How else would you spell it?" I had asked, innocently.

"With an IE." She didn't say, "You asshole." She didn't have to.

"Oh."

I sat down on the bed nearest the door. Stacy had taken the one near the window. Fair is fair, I thought. She got here first.

Stacy with a Y turned back to her dresser. She was wearing very short shorts, showing off her great legs. She flexed her thigh muscles as she started to unpack about a thousand leotards. How did she do that? She was flexing her thigh muscles without moving her calf muscles!

"So," she turned back to me, "do you dance?"

Nothing this Stacy with a Y said made any sense to me. "Do I dance?" I felt like I had been condemned to spend the next year repeating everything she said.

She smiled, with a C (for condescending). "I'm a modern dancer. I live to dance."

"That's nice."

"I guess you don't," she said. "Too bad." She turned back to her unpacking. "It's SO good for the figure, you know."

I squeezed my fat thighs together—my calf muscles flexed at the same time—and sucked in my tummy. Great. I was going to feel like a blob in my new home away from home.

"I like swimming," I said to her back.

"Swimming's good exercise, but it won't shape you up the way dance will." She turned back to me, stretched her right leg out in front of her, pointed her right toe, and raised her leg straight up over her head. "See? Dancing makes you SO limber." She kept her leg up there, and rounded her arms up over her head too. How did she do that? Then she smiled at me again. "I could teach you some stretching exercises. I have a superior turn-out. All my teachers tell me that. Ever since I was little. I could help you." She put her arms and leg back down into normal-land. "I couldn't teach you how to have such a good turn-out. That's innate. But I could teach you a few stretches."

"Thanks," I said. Just what I needed. A turn-out tune up from a born ballerina. "I stretch after I swim." Good way to start with a new roommate. Lie your head off. Well, it was better than having her on my case about increasing my turn-out, whatever that was. And I wasn't going to ask her. Enough is enough.

"This is my boyfriend, Todd," she said, picking up a silver frame with a picture of a guy so good-looking he looked like he came with the frame. "Isn't he soo cute?"

"Yes," I said.

"Soon we'll be Todd and Stacy Monroe. Doesn't that sound so great? Stacy Monroe."

With a Y.

"Do you have a boyfriend?" she asked, hugging the picture of Todd to her breasts.

"No," I said.

"Too bad. Well, there are lots of mixers to go to."

Mixers? Not on your life. I would NEVER go to a mixer.

"You'll find somebody." She turned her back to me again. I had failed the Stacy—with a Y—initial interview.

Oh, shut up about Stacy. Who cares about Stacy? You need to find someone you can talk to, not someone whose each and every body part evokes unspeakable envy. Keep the pen moving. Look around the room as you write down everything.

What did Ms. Rosenberg just say about footnotes? God, she's been talking about footnotes for an hour!

Anyone look like a possible friend? Don't even think about how you would ever get to meet her, talk to her. Forget that. Just look. Look and keep writing. "Twenty-page research paper." Amazing how Ms. Rosenberg's words can flow through my pen and onto my paper and leave not a trace of anything in my brain.

There must be at least one other girl who doesn't know anyone. People don't all go to college with their friends. I can't be the only one.

That one over there, she looks like a possibility. Nice cheekbones, great red hair, doodling in her notebook. No, probably not. Too sophisticated, too cool. She looks like one of those girls who grew up reading the *New York Review of Books* and knows everything about twentieth-century American literature. Why would she want to be friends with me, who can't even get through the first paragraph of an article in the *New York Times*? Forget her. What? God, I missed that last sentence. Something about our assignment.

"What did she say?" the girl next to me whispered.

"I didn't hear it," I whispered back.

And then that girl did the most incredible thing—she

actually raised her hand and asked Ms. Rosenberg to repeat what she had just said! I was amazed, awestruck. And Ms. Rosenberg repeated it, just as if it were normal, and wrote it on the board. Well, what did you think was going to happen? That hairy patches would appear on Ms. Rosenberg's arms and face, she would start to howl, turn into a werewolf, latch onto the poor girl's neck and start feeding on her flesh?

Here's the thing. I have never talked in class. Not in grade school, not in high school. Sure, I gave my oral reports. I could READ aloud in class. I just couldn't TALK aloud in class.

Write down the assignment, you dip. When is it due? Must be next week. Has to be next week.

"Ms. Rosenberg, did you say the assignment was due next week?" That girl again. That same girl. Maybe if I brush by her on the way out, touch her arm with my arm, some of her bravery will rub off. Maybe if I dress like her. Jeans torn at the knees, good knees, not perfect, but strong. Soft pink T-shirt, very worn. Cozy. Great hair. Really great hair. Not perfect, like Stacy's. Soft. Natural. Stacy's is not natural. It's man-made, artificial. Stacy-made. This one's is flowing, curly, but it goes all which-a-way. A mind of its own. Her hair has a mind of its own.

"Yes, Ruth. It's due next week."

Normal, a normal conversation. Plain vanilla real life. I could use a big dose of that. Me, I'm shocked when I walk into one of those old-fashioned stores that has a mat inside the door and when you step on it, the bell rings. I'm always surprised that it rings when *I* walk in. Me? It rang for me? It noticed that I stepped on it?

What is the assignment that's due next week? Oh, God, I hope I wrote it down. There's the bell. Great. You know something's due next week, but you don't know what it is. Say something to that girl. Ruth. She seems nice. Say something. Say something before she walks out. Too late. Oh. It's up there on the board. The assignment is staring you in the face. Write it down. Just write it down.

Okay. What's your next class? You can't burst into tears in the middle of Euclid Hall. You'll have to wait till later. Cry tomorrow. Go to your next class—now. Write down everything. Look around the room. Try and find a friend.

God, I don't understand a word this man is saying. Why am I taking Geology? I was never interested in rocks, or soil, or whatever he is talking about. Is that girl Ruth in this class? That would be nice. No, she's not. Shit. Everyone looks like they understand what he is saying. Read the book, he is saying. Then you'll understand everything. Good. That's a help. Maybe you don't need to listen. What book? The textbook. The assigned text. Look at the bibliography he passed out. Oh, good. He wrote the textbook. His lectures are probably just cribbed from his own book. Can you plagiarize from yourself? Shut up! I can't listen to you anymore.

It is exhausting living here, inside of this maniac. This lonely maniac. I never felt this way before. I was never in this situation before—all alone, with no one I knew. Why didn't I think of this before I applied to college? Or at least before I decided to go here. Alone. Without a single friend, or even acquaintance.

Oh, my God, it's not true! I have been in this situation before! When I was twelve and my parents took me on a vacation to Florida, I stayed in the motel room for the entire week that we were there. I don't remember anything except that there were all kinds of kids running around the pool right outside my window. They all seemed to know each other.

"Go out there and make friends," my mother had said. She had said it again and again.

Sure. Just go out there, into a big group of kids who had grown up together, who all knew each other, who didn't need another kid in their pool. Sure. I had stayed inside, curtains drawn and played solitaire the whole time we were there. When I would close my eyes at night, cards would float before my eyes. Kings, queens, jacks. Red and black. And when I woke up in the morning, I would play some more.

Why hadn't I thought of that before I decided to go to a school where I knew no one? Why hadn't I remembered that horrible vacation?

Maybe I should start writing. That always helped when I was little, when I was home alone because I was sick and couldn't have anyone come over because I would infect them with my germs. When I was seven, I wrote a story about germs—big gelatinous germs that flew around the sick person's head and hissed and stuck their tongues out at healthy people, blowing their diseases at anyone who came close. The germs were having a good time. And they weren't mean—they were just germs, doing their job—making people sick. Nancy, the main character, made friends with the germs. The one she liked best was named Sven. He was the funniest one. The others had names too—Helena, Georgida, Antoine, Jeannine, Rolfe. I don't remember the rest.

But the germs didn't want to leave, they were having such a good time with Nancy. And Nancy wasn't getting any better, no matter what her parents and her doctor did. Nancy didn't care, because she was having fun with her germs. They were very bright, and appreciative of the pictures she drew and the stories she wrote. They loved everything she did. In the end, Nancy went off to live in germ-land, with her best friends, the germs.

Maybe I should write a story about a girl who fell in love with her own brain. Who decided there was no one else worth talking to. Just a girl and her mind. Do your homework. You might as well be a good student before you go totally off the deep end.

* * *

Two days later, I was no better as I walked into English class. Ruth was sitting there already. I slunk into the seat next to her, the same seat I had had two days ago.

"Hi," she said to me. And smiled.

"Hi," I said. I tried to smile. My mouth didn't feel like it was working very well, since I hadn't used it to do anything but eat for the past two weeks. I hoped my lips were going up at the ends.

Ms. Rosenberg walked in and took her place behind the desk. I opened my notebook and poised my pen over a blank page. A blank page. An open book. A beginning. Enough high drama, Naomi. Shut up and listen.

Ruth poked me. "Did you start on the assignment yet?" she whispered.

"No," I whispered back.

Ms. Rosenberg looked daggers at us and we both shut up. She started talking and I started writing. I saw Ruth's hand moving out of the corner of my eye. It was moving oddly. Not like writing movements. More jerky, less controlled. I peeked at her notebook. She wasn't taking notes at all! She was drawing—naked people! Big faces with long hair cascading down their naked shoulders. Curly hair, straight hair. The faces were different. But everyone was buck naked. Breasts, big and small, butts, some large, others perky, vaginas, hairy and shaved. And there were men too! Erect penises, flaccid penises, giant ones, tiny ones, balls the size of grapefruits, balls the size of marbles, some bodies almost completely covered with hair, others smooth as babies.

My hand stopped writing. It held my pen poised over the paper, but it didn't move at all. I looked up at Ruth. She smiled at me. I tried to smile and realized my mouth was hanging open. I shut it and smiled.

Oh, my God. Should I be smiling? Is she some kind of pervert? Was my smile encouraging some sexual advance? Did she run orgies in her dorm room? Where had she seen so many different kinds of bodies? Was she drawing from personal experience, simultaneous or serial? Who was this woman? And why didn't the bell ring?

I didn't look up again until the period was over. I just wrote. My blank page and the next one were full of blue scribbles. I wondered if I would be able to read them once I got back to my room.

The bell rang. My hand was exhausted.

"You take such good notes," Ruth said as she picked up her books.

"Yeah," I said. "It helps me pay attention." Maybe *you* should try it.

"Paying attention is sooo hard," Ruth said. "Once I went to the bathroom and soaked my underpants in cold water to get through my Senior Physics class. God, I hated that class so much. The wet underpants kept me awake."

Did some weirdo suggest it to her? Before or after they took off all their clothes and danced around?

"Didn't the wet leak through?" I blurted out.

Ruth laughed. "Yes. It sure did. Why weren't you there to warn me then?"

Why indeed. Because I wouldn't have gotten near you. Because I'm not the type to be seen bare naked—or even bare breasted—in public. But she was nice. Funny. Soaking her underpants in cold water. Well, it was a good idea.

She tossed her hair back and picked up her books. "What room are you in? I might need to check something in those elegant notes of yours."

"Hewitt five sixty-seven."

"Cool. I'm in Hewitt seven ninety-four. See ya."

"See ya." Did I need this strange person as a friend? Was I that desperate? Maybe.

The weekend. Here comes the weekend. Friday afternoon, the grayest sky in the world, and it's my last class. The weekend is the worst. All the girls who have boyfriends are psyched to go out with them. All the girls who don't are psyched to go to mixers. Weekends are the worst. No classes I have to go to. No nothing I have to do. No place I have to be. Just me alone. Still alone.

Sunday morning. Stacy had a big date Saturday night. She'd made friends with some girls in her modern dance class. Stacy and one of those other perfect girls had their boyfriends in town for the weekend and the two of them chattered on and on all morning, while I pretended to still be asleep, covers over my head.

"Isn't Todd the cutest thing you have ever seen? He has the cutest butt."

"Todd has a cute butt, but Jason is premed." This from Kimberly—also with a Y.

"I can't believe we both have our dream guys in for the weekend. Todd is soooo cute. Isn't it great that they are best friends and we are best friends!"

They both squealed and probably hugged each other. Or maybe they took ballerina poses.

"Let's go find them. They said they'd be at Reggie's," Stacy said. And they left.

You didn't used to hate people so much, Naomi. This isn't good for you. You used to have a sense of humor. You used to have fun.

This is not Florida, Naomi. You are not an idiot pre-adolescent, mad at your parents for taking you on a vacation you didn't want to go on. You are seventeen. You can drive, you can almost drink. You are the boss of yourself, now. I think you better fix this. I think you have to DO something.

I walked up the two flights of stairs to the seventh floor, my notebook under my arm. I was going to say I didn't understand Ms. Rosenberg's English assignment—and that I never take my clothes off. Never. Seven ninety-four must be at the opposite end of the hall. I have never walked so slowly in my life. You're not going to be executed, Naomi. You're walking down this hall to make a friend. If she's got a room full of naked people, you can walk away. You're walking down this hall to get your life back to normal, so you can laugh and think happy thoughts. You are walking down this hall because you need to. Shut up about all the walking!

I stood in front of 794. Knock. Just knock. Do it already.

I knocked.

No answer.

I knocked again.

No answer.

Whew. She's not there. I don't have to do this. Shit, she's not there. I'm going to have to do it all over again later. Shit shit shit. I stood there, staring at the door, half relieved, half pissed. Okay. You did it once, you can do it again. Maybe it'll be easier the next time. Chill. Come back later.

I walked up the two flights again. I walked down the hall and stood in front of 794 again. She won't be there now, either. At least you have something to do now. Walk up two flights of stairs, walk down a hall, and stare at a door. Good exercise, right Stacy? The door opened. I almost hit Ruth in the head with my raised knocking fist. She was dressed. Whew.

"Sorry," I said.

"It's you! I've been looking all over for you! I forgot your room number."

"You're Naomi?" someone from inside the room asked. She came toward the door. "Hi! I'm Eileen."

She had clothes on too. Thank you, God.

"My roommate," Ruth said. "Come on in! Sit." She gestured to the bed and sat back down at her desk.

"I was just going down to the machines to get some

sodas," said Eileen. "Want a Coke or anything?"

"Sure," I said. I started to dig into my pants pockets for some change.

"Forget it," said Eileen. "You can get the next round."

The next round, I thought. There would be a next round? Would I have to take my clothes off for the next round?

"Yeah," said Ruth. "Get us some Cokes while we look at the assignment and then we could all go to the park and draw. It's so nice and I haven't been out all day."

Draw in the park? Was there a nude beach out there in Riverside Park?

I looked out the window. It *was* nice out. Sunny, clear sky. I hadn't even noticed.

"Great. I'll be right back," said Eileen. She left.

"I am sooo lucky to have her for a roommate. She wrote me a letter over the summer and I thought we'd never get along. She's all into science stuff and I just want to draw—plants, animals, anything."

"You draw all kinds of things?" I asked, trying to look innocent.

"Yeah. Anything. I took a lot of life drawing classes over the summer so I'm still into that."

Oh my God! Drawing classes! Classes where models pose naked! Places to see many naked bodies! Many different naked bodies! Oh.

"But I really like doing landscapes," Ruth was saying. "And I thought Eileen'd be like, 'Oh, that's nice, yeah, that's pretty, but right now I'm VERY busy with figuring out how to cure cancer.' But then I met her. I knew the minute we met it would be okay. You know, that thing in your brain that goes YES, or NO, like instantly. Know what I mean?"

"Yeah," I said. "Your Sproing."

"What?"

Why did you just blurt that out, you idiot? Now she thinks you're the psycho.

But she didn't look like she thought I was a psycho.

She looked like she wanted to know what I meant.

"Your Sproing—Sproing I hate her, Sproing I like her."

Was that clear? Would she get it?

"My Sproing," Ruth said. "Exactly." She smiled.

Whew. Exactly. She got it. I knew she would. I smiled back.

Rachel's Vampire

Paul Zindel

My years in high school were ones I've drawn upon often as inspiration throughout my writing career. There were so many phantasmagoric and exciting and frightening corners of my heart in which all kinds of secrets and dreams were able to hide.

More than anything, I remember high school as a time of yearning. There was much I wanted to say, so many classmates I wanted to tell my secret feelings to—but I was too shy or cowardly. In high school, I met the life models (my inspiration homunculi) that often have populated my fiction, my dozens of plays and novels and movies. But there were many others, fascinating kids who were like smaller canvasses, supernumeraries for whom I have yet to find a place. It is from the vapors of memory that one girl has returned from that amazing and irreplaceable Time:

"Write about me," she seems to whisper. "Now."

Rachel arrived at my school at a time when children were being sent north from Cuba and other exotic countries of fomenting political danger to safety in American orphanages. Oh, there were euphemisms for the Homes, but orphanages they were. Hundreds of such kids came to live for a while at the Presentation Home on Staten Island and attend my public school. Presentation Home was an unsettling, audacious adventure. Appalling stories flowed with regularity from the orphanage, tales of cruel and athletic and terrifying happenings. A group of Presentation Home girls tried to hurl a young woman counselor off its oceanside cliff. Another time, when I was in a car passing through the orphanage grounds, I watched paralyzed as a dozen of the Home boys dragged a giant turtle onto the asphalt basketball court and butchered it with a shovel.

Many of the kids living at the Home were regular, even gifted—like Rachel, who had been shipped from South America. These brighter, academic students were allowed to leave the Home for the day to attend classes at my local public high school. It was there that I met and got to know Rachel. She was my partner on school trips to places like the Brooklyn Museum, and the Franklin Institute in Philadelphia. Once we stood looking at an exhibit of intricately carved antique wooden chests, and she sighed. "Oh, this is what people did before they had television."

For several months, Rachel and I confronted steam tables together and ate our lunches in my school's cafeteria. It was Rachel de la Mayo who told me the account that follows. It's the true story of a lesson she learned about—well, she said it was about her dating—going steady with a native boy far up in the rain forest of the Amazon jungle. It had to do with intense feelings of a girl for a boy, and how she managed to recover from a hurting heart. I've often remembered it as a dram of the true elixir of wisdom that had come crashing in upon her during an internship on her father's expedition along a remote tributary of the Amazon. It's a tutelage in healing the human heart and battling the vampires of our lives—a tale I could never forget. So I tell you her story now.

Rachel saw the vampire coming for her, hurtling down from the cosmos with a legion of night herons. Tarantulas and fat beetles clawed at her, began to break her skin. The vampire seized her in the light of a full moon. She tried to run, but a blanket of ticks rained down onto her and became the vampire's wings. The bat-thing was hot and wet with fresh blood, and it opened its mouth to . . .

Rachel screamed.

She woke up trembling and saw Moduro, brown and glaring, standing in the doorway of her tent. He gave her a moment to calm down and wipe away the scarf of sweat that had tightened about her neck.

The dream of the vampire still gripped her.

"I have come to tell you that we won't meet or love

each other any longer," Moduro said. "Our love is over. The time has come for me to marry a girl from my tribe and to say good-bye to you. Our lifetimes will never touch again. You will not speak of me, and I will not speak of you. You must not think of me. Our Time together is dead."

Rachel began to cry, tears spilling from her immense green eyes. She lifted herself from the scoop of her cot and brushed her thick brown hair to one side as a shield. She had no words for Moduro, only thoughts: *Every day until I die I will dream of you. I will remember what it was like to love my first boy and have him love me in return.*

She watched Moduro turn and swagger away. She stood, pulled a robe around herself, and walked barefoot on the damp straw. From the open flap of her tent, she watched her young man disappear into a wall of vines and the eternal mist that drifted down through the rain forest. She knew he would follow the river, the great river that had been born in the Andes and that would soon flood the forest as it did every year.

Now the voices of her father and his workers drifted down from the canopy above. Her father's tones, scholarly and scientific. And Curas, the foreman and shaman, his voice gentle with a mix of Portuguese and Amazonian. Above all, there was the sound of machetes cutting back the highest mahogany branches to keep vines from creeping onto the catwalk.

Rachel reached the river bank. She had known the time for love to end had been coming. She knew she was temporary, that Moduro's marriage to the girl from his tribe had been planned for several years. The union would give him a place in the only universe he knew, his remote and dangerous and unforgiving jungle tribe.

I gave you adoration and trinkets and dazzled you with thoughts you would have never known. For a while, I was like a fire to you. Rousing. Burning. She grasped her sides from the pain. She couldn't let go.

Couldn't.

But everything in the jungle changed. Always. That was the way it was. The waters would rise and fish would swim in the forest. Giant ferns would arise where her father's camp stood, and great schools of piranha and eels would appear. River dolphins had already begun to play near the falls, and Spider monkeys chattered frantically in the silver bark trees. Her time as an intern was to end soon, but she would demand to leave now.

"Father!" Rachel wiped at her tears and shouted up to the canopy. "I want to go home. Please let me go home!"

The next morning her father instructed three of his best river men to stock a dugout and prepare to take his daughter on the long downriver journey to Manaus. The men had made the journey many times. He knew she would be safe. Curas, an old buffalo of a shaman, his head thrust forward between his shoulders, helped Rachel put together a first-aid kit with syringes and medicines to fight snake bites or malaria flare-ups.

"I dreamed a ghastly vampire would come for me," she confided to the shaman. "Do you think it was Moduro telling me our love is over?"

Curas saw the tears in her eyes. "What I am afraid of is that the vampire was not Moduro. That the vampire you dreamed of will be waiting for you on the river."

Rachel saw the alarm in Curas' eyes, and it made panic draw her belly into a knot. She had seen Curas troubleshoot problems for her father, knew that he had the special gift of clairvoyance. He would know across great distances, without phone or walkie-talkie, when one of his men or children had stepped on a python or had fallen from a tree.

"I'll be careful," Rachel promised.

"Yes," the old man said. "You must be very careful."

Rachel waved good-bye to her father and Curas, and to the workers high in the canopy. Their women were smiling below, churning pots of grains mixed with their saliva and tapir's milk. The smiles stayed upon their faces until the boat started around the river bend.

Yes, Rachel told herself, settling low in the dugout, the vampire from her dream had to be Moduro. She began to pray with malice. With anguish and the poison of bad dreams and a thirst for vengeance.

Am I supposed to forget how much I loved you? You were all I ever wanted. Do I pretend I never knew you?

The Indians with her in the boat were Curdaruci, short, dark, with powerful builds and shiny straight black hair. They cut their paddles into the river with the sharpness of knives, and used them as rudders in the rapids. Dusk set in and the sky reddened. Aruanas began to leap above the giant water lilies. The fish were comical, sometimes frightful, nearly always enormous.

Torda, with a broken front tooth and midnight hair to his waist, picked their camping spot for the night and supervised the raising of the tents and making of the fires. At each waterfall, they all pitched in to carry the long pirogue dugout carefully down to the next stretch of flat, slow river.

"There will be rocks and whitewater and twenty-nine waterfalls," Torda said.

Rachel said, "Thank you for preparing me."

Are you the vampire, she had wanted to ask Torda and both of the other men. *Is one of you my vampire?* She wanted to tell them about her nightmare so she could sleep or laugh or expect to die. She thought about announcing straight out that she knew one of them was a vampire and that she would like to get it all over with. She thought about shouting the accusation and watching their eyes for guilt.

Their hands.

Their legs.

"Have you ever dreamed of vampires?" she asked instead.

Torda translated her words. The three men laughed. When they saw she was serious, the smiles left their faces. Yes, they had seen many vampire bats on trees that lay across the tributaries and lacework of swamps. Small bats that bite into the necks of sleeping men and monkeys and wild boars.

Yes, the three of them have many bad dreams of vampires, Torda told her. And bad dreams of pumas attacking them in the trees and giant cayman alligators twisting, turning, dragging them under the surface of the river. Fears of tree spirits and mountain lightning and tiny catfish that can swim into their bodies.

None of you are the vampire of which I dreamed. Rachel decided. Instead, her thoughts returned to Moduro and the pain of thinking about him numbed her into asleep.

The next day, the river was deeper, and flowed much too fast. The jungle itself became a tapestry of orchids and balsa trees swollen with red and purple parrots.

Each evening she would not forget the vampire of her dream, the flying beast from the moonlit sky with its rain of ticks and a mouth of fangs. She remained alert, on watch, knowing deep inside of her that it might still come.

The third afternoon the dugout approached an Indian malorca, a small tribe area at the edge of the river. Rachel's eyes were drawn to the long mud beach in front of the village. Nearly forty Indians had come down to the bank. There were men with straw woven into their hair, and women with moonstones strung as necklaces and holding children in their arms. Boys played tag.

Closer Rachel noticed what looked like glistening scarlet packets strewn out on the bank. Rachel saw fear gripping her men. She heard it in Torda's voice. Something was wrong.

The shining slabs on the beach were raw meat. Meat and bone like that of butchered . . .

Rachel saw the unmistakable remains of human hands and feet. At the center of the slaughter lay the severed head of a woman. Rachel turned her face away from the sight.

Her nightmare was here.

"Stop," she shouted at Torda. "I want to know what happened," Rachel said. "Ask them."

The men paddled the boat slowly into the shallows, but held their paddles ready. Torda called to the villagers, and a shaman came forward from the crowd and answered Torda in his language.

"Who killed these people?" Rachel shouted.

Torda motioned her to be patient. When he understood everything the shaman had to say, he spoke to her. "The slaughtered men and women were a family. The village had to kill them because they were about to change into winged beasts. The shaman says that is what happens every few years. A family in the village begins to change into monsters that would destroy the village if they lived. The slaughtered family had begun its metamorphosis."

Rachel heard a sound coming from the slaughter. A baby moved in the mud near one woman's body. Before Torda could stop her, Rachel was out of the boat and wading toward the bank. She picked up the baby and cradled it. Its umbilical cord dropped away.

The village's warrior men moved toward Rachel.

Rachel ordered Torda, "Tell the shaman I'll take the baby far away and they'll never see it again. If the baby does change into a monster, it will be me that it will attack."

Without waiting for an answer, Rachel carried the baby to the pirogue and climbed in. "Get us out of here," she said.

Torda spoke gently to the shaman and the villagers, as he and the other two men began to paddle. Rachel knew he was calming them. Assuring them. She will take the baby away. Far away . . .

Soon, the pirogue was back safely in the middle of the river and heading fast downstream once more. The baby was crying.

Screaming.

Clawing at her shirt.

"I know you're hungry," Rachel said, softly. She knew all the food that they had packed for themselves was salted strips of tapir and boar. There was nothing aboard for a newborn to eat. Nothing that wouldn't kill it. She asked Torda if he or the men knew of anything in the jungle that the baby could eat.

There was nothing. "Indian babies die if there is no mother's milk," Torda said.

Rachel leaned forward to keep the sun off the little boy. Its cries of hunger were shrill now. A howl to live. She could see the baby's lips were cracked and dry and trembling. Rachel began to cry. For a few moments, her sobs racked her body. Her tongue felt thick and her eyes burned from the scorching light. She felt the mud drying on her legs, and she glimpsed death trying to crawl into the baby's eyes.

Is this another death I must accept? Rachel wondered. Is the death of babies and love something she must agree to? Just let them go? Let love and life go?

She grasped the baby and balanced it on her knee while she searched through the sack of provisions. There was nothing that wouldn't be poison for a baby. She opened the first-aid kit and stared at the syringes and bandage rolls and vials of pills. For a moment she clutched one of the packaged syringes. Torda said nothing as she suddenly tore its cover away. Quickly, Rachel had the syringe's needle into a vein of her arm. Her dark-red blood filled the glass tube.

She lay the wailing infant back into the cradle of her arms. She took a rubber glove from the kit, cut off one of its "fingers," and pierced it with a needle.

"This is the food I've got for you," Rachel said, as she slipped the makeshift nipple gently into the baby's mouth. The baby stopped crying. He looked up at her, staring into her eyes. The look of death disappeared from his eyes as she covered his maleness with her shirt tail. When she felt his heartbeat beneath the palms of her hands, she felt a warmth begin to surround her heart.

The hotness touched her throat and then her face and mind.

Slowly.

It was like awakening.

A spiraling upward. She found herself whispering to the baby. "I, too, will live. I will live and forget—and love again."

She heard Torda and the men laughing.

"What is it?" she asked.

"The baby," Torda said, watching the baby suckle her blood. "We have given him a name. He is your vampire. He is Rachel's Vampire."

Carefully, Rachel let one hand dip into the river. She gently brushed drops of its coolness onto the baby's brow and temples and through his hair.

"Are you? Is that who you are?" She smiled. "Are you my little vampire?"

ABOUT THE CONTRIBUTORS

JOAN ABELOVE is the author of two novels for young adults, *Go and Come Back* (1998), an American Library Association Notable Children's Book, ALA/YALSA Best Book for Young Adults, *Publishers Weekly* Best Book of the Year, and *Los Angeles Times* Book Prize finalist, and *Saying It Out Loud* (1999), a *Publishers Weekly* Best Book of the Year. *Sproing!* is her first short story. Joan lives in New York City with her husband and son.

MEL GLENN is the author of twelve books for young adults, including *Jump Ball, Foreign Exchange,* and *Who Killed Mr. Chippendale?*, which was nominated for the prestigious Edgar Allan Poe Award of the Mystery Writers of America. He has received the Christopher Award and the Golden Kite Honor Award, and the American Library Association has recognized several of his titles as Best Books for Young Adults. In addition, the ALA named his *Who Killed Mr. Chippendale?* one of the Top Ten Books of the Year.

Mr. Glenn was born in Zurich, Switzerland, and grew up in Brooklyn, New York, and teaches English at his alma mater, Lincoln High School. He and his wife, Elyse, live in Brooklyn. They have two sons, Jonathan and Andrew.

ADELE GRIFFIN is the author of a number of books for young readers, including *Sons of Liberty*, a National Book Award Finalist and ALA Best Book for Young Adults and *The Other Shepards*, an ALA Notable Book and *Publishers Weekly* and *School Library Journal* Best Book of the Year. She lives in New York City.

JOYCE HANSEN was born and raised in New York City, the setting of her early contemporary novels. She received a bachelor's degree from Pace University and completed graduate work at New York University where she earned an Master's degree in English Education. Ms. Hansen was a teacher and staff developer in the New York City public school system for twenty-two years. She has also taught writing and literature at Empire State College (SUNY). In 1995 she retired from teaching and presently lives near Columbia, South Carolina, where she writes full-time.

Joyce Hansen has published short stories and twelve books of contemporary and historical fiction and nonfiction for young readers. She has won the Coretta Scott King Honor Book Award four times and the 1999 Carter G. Woodson Secondary Honor Book Award sponsored by the National Council for the Social Studies.

DAVID LUBAR is a writer and video game programmer. His nine books include the novel *Hidden Talents,* an ALA Best Books for Young Adults selection, and the Psychozone story collections. Among the forty games he's coded are Home Alone and Frogger for the Game Boy. A bit over a quarter century ago he went to Morristown High School in New Jersey where he got along just fine with the majority of the wrestlers. He only fenced for one year, then dropped all school sports to study karate. But that's another story.

MARY ANN McGUIGAN's first novel for young adults, *Cloud Dancer*, was published by Scribner's Sons in 1994. Her second, *Where You Belong*, published by Atheneum in 1997 and set in the Bronx neighborhood where she was born, was a finalist for the National Book Award for Young People's Literature. Both novels were selected for the New York Public Library's Best Books for the Teen Age. Mary Ann's short stories written for adult readers appeared during the 1980s in small-press publications. A former high school English teacher, Mary Ann is now managing editor of *Wealth Manager* magazine, a Bloomberg publication. She lives in New Jersey.

LOIS METZGER is the author of the novels *Barry's Sister* (a *Parents* magazine Best Book of the Year) and *Ellen's Case* (a New York Public Library Book for the Teenaged). Her most recent novel is *Missing Girls* (a Junior Library Guild Book). She lives in New York City with her husband, writer Tony Hiss, and their son, Jacob.

TAMORA PIERCE has fifteen fantasy novels for teenagers in print in English worldwide and in German, Swedish and Danish language translation as of spring 2000. Many of her books have appeared on numerous year's best lists. She lives in Manhattan with her husband, technical writer/webpage designer Tim Liebe, and their three cats and two budgies, most of whom are rescued animals.

JON SCIESZKA went to high school for four years, taught junior high school for a few years, and always handed in his writing assignments on time . . . more or less. He wrote and published the very successful *True Story of the 3 Little Pigs!, The Stinky Cheese Man, Squids Will Be Squids,* and a bunch of other stuff, proving that sometimes procrastinating does pay.

SHELLEY STOEHR is the author of four acclaimed novels for young adults: *Crosses, Weird on the Outside, Wannabe* and *Tomorrow Wendy. Crosses,* published while Shelley was a student at Connecticut College, is an ALA Recommended Book for Reluctant Young Readers an ALA Best Book for Young Adults, and a YALSA Popular Paperbacks for Young Adults, 1999.

Stoehr has appeared as an expert on the Maury Povich show, and on numerous radio shows to talk about self-injuring, or "cutting" (the subject matter of *Crosses*).

Shelley Stoehr now lives in Pomona, California with her fiancée, Chris, and two dogs, Bone and Max.

ELEANORA E. TATE is the author of many middle-grade books, including her newest, *African American Mu-*

sicians, The Secret of Gumbo Grove (a Parents Choice Gold Seal Award winner featured on National Public Radio's "All Things Considered") and its sister book, *Thank You, Dr. Martin Luther King, Jr.!* (an NCSS-CBC Notable Children's Trade Book in the Field of Social Studies). *Just an Overnight Guest* was the basis for an award-winning film of the same name. Tate's short stories and essays have appeared in *American Girl, Book Links*, and *Goldfinch* magazines, and in *African American Review*. She is a 1999 recipient of a distinguished Zora Neale Hurston award from the National Association of Black Storytellers, Inc., and a Bread Loaf Literary Fellow.

RICH WALLACE is the author of two novels for teenagers, *Wrestling Sturbridge* and *Shots on Goal*, both published by Alfred A. Knopf. A third novel is scheduled for publication in the fall of 2000. Rich grew up in a small town in Bergen County, New Jersey, and has participated in sports throughout his life. He spent several years as a sports writer and editor, and is now a senior editor at *Highlights for Children* magazine. He lives in Honesdale, Pennsylvania, with his two sons, Jonathan and Jeremy.

PAUL ZINDEL is an award-winning playwright as well as the author some of the most popular and critically praised novels for young adults. He was born in Staten Island, New York. Although he wrote his first play while still in high school, he attended Wagner College and majored in chemistry. While at college he studied with playwright Edward Albee. After college he worked as a technical writer for a time and also taught high school chemistry for ten years. But he continued writing plays. His first staged play—*The Effect of Gamma Rays on Man-in-the-Moon Marigolds*—won the Pulitzer Prize for Drama and was turned into a successful motion picture.

His novels for young people include *The Pigman*, A Boston Globe-Horn Book Award and Child Study Association of America's Children's Books of the Year Award winner,

The Effect of Gamma Rays on Man-in-the-Moon Marigolds, an American Library Association Best Book for Young Adult, *Pardon Me, You're Stepping on My Eyeball; Confessions of a Teenage Baboon;* and *The Pigman's Legacy.*

He lives in New Jersey.